THE F

"The shift between this world and a strange, parallel world grips you and, like so much good fantasy, teases you with unknown possibilities. The way the other world intrudes is both dramatic and chilling." *Books for Keeps*

Fear and suspense are important ingredients in Hugh Scott's books – but then what would you expect from the Master of Menace? "Atmosphere is vital," he says, "especially in books about the supernatural. I try to make my books scary." He doesn't believe, though, in gratuitous horror. "I wouldn't indulge myself in things that were revolting or disgusting," he says. "It's boring, self-indulgent and unnecessary. Everything you write should advance the story."

It was in 1984, two years after winning the Woman's Realm Children's Story Writing Competition that Hugh Scott decided to give up his job as an art teacher and become a full-time writer. His first novel, *The Shaman's Stone*, was published in 1988 and several more titles soon followed. These include *Why Weeps the Brogan?* (winner of the 1989 Whitbread Children's Novel Award), *The Haunted Sand*, *Something Watching*, *The Gargoyle* and *A Ghost Waiting*.

Hugh Scott is married with two grown-up children and lives in Scotland.

Books by the same author

A Box of Tricks
The Camera Obscura
Freddie and the Enormouse
The Gargoyle
A Ghost Waiting
The Haunted Sand
Something Watching
Why Weeps the Brogan?

For younger readers

Change the King!
The Summertime Santa

THE PLACE BETWEEN

HUGH SCOTT

WALKER BOOKS
AND SUBSIDIARIES

LONDON • BOSTON • SYDNEY

First published 1994 by Walker Books Ltd
87 Vauxhall Walk, London SE11 5HJ

This edition published 1995

2 4 6 8 10 9 7 5 3 1

This book has been typeset in Sabon.

Printed in England

British Library Cataloguing in Publication Data
A catalogue record for this book is available from
the British Library.

ISBN 0-7445-3680-4

This book is for Leslie Taylor,
with my thanks for our adventures
in and around Gloucestershire.

"What I want," said Dr Johnson, *"is an explanation for just about every ghost that ever was."*

Buckingham Palace,
London SW1A 1AA

Her Majesty the Queen,

                    Grimshaw's Farm,
                    Rent Lane
                    Lowcester GL12 2AX

                    28th July 1994

Madam,

I am sorry to bother you with my troubles, as I'm sure you have plenty to do without concerning yourself about me, but my husband is no help, seeing that he believes in nothing beyond crops and cows – and Bernie Kemp just isn't scared enough to worry. But, Your Majesty, I am getting very nervous about what's happening around Bosky Wood.

Bosky Wood is a stone's throw from my farm. Down the lane from our farmhouse is the main road, which goes left to Lowcester and right towards Oxford (though it's not a real main road, of course, being too narrow) – and across that road is Bosky Wood.

The wood has had a bad reputation in these parts for generations, but it seems to me that things are worse in recent years, and getting worse still, as if some Power was at work.

I won't trouble you, Ma'am, with the long story of my husband's grandfather – for that was twenty years ago – but I must mention that Able (my husband) came into our kitchen about nine years back with the strangest look on his face. I knew something odd had happened, because if it had been something ordinary to do with the building of the new barn, he would have said. Bernie Kemp knew, but he wouldn't talk about it because Able wouldn't – to save me from worrying, I expect.

My husband having a look on his face isn't much of a story, Ma'am, but if you knew him, you'd know it meant something. He still hasn't told me what it was about.

Then five years ago, a family arrived in a car at my door, asking the way to Oxford, and I said, "Go back down the lane and turn right."

The man looked at me as if not liking to argue. His wife, too, seemed unwilling to speak. Then one of the children – I think it was a little girl – said, "But it's all trees." And I said again, "Go down the lane and turn right," thinking that the child was just being a child. But the man put his hand on the little girl's head, and said politely enough, "The road ends among the trees. That's why we came up the lane to your house."

Well, I couldn't make it out at all, him saying that the road to Oxford ended among trees – and you can imagine how the conversation ding-donged (in the nicest way, for they were a right nice family), but eventually I went down to the main road with them and pointed them to the right, and I can assure you, Ma'am, that the man and woman turned as white as a bucket of milk, and the little girls were mighty upset, for the road went clear away to the right as surely as it approached from the left. All this was in broad daylight.

In 1988, Able (my husband) cut down the oak trees on the mound. The mound is a slightly raised bit of ground with some old stones on it, in the pasture beside Bosky Wood, and it is just a step or two *from* the wood. The trees which grew among the stones had come up crooked – though old and strong – so Able had them cut into fencing (them being little use for anything else) and used the fencing to contain Bosky Wood, because any wood – as Your Majesty knows, owning so much property and taking such an interest in it – can spread, if you don't decide on a boundary and stick to it.

The spare timber, after the fencing was cut, we used as firewood, being – as I said – misshapen. But the strange thing that happened, Ma'am, was while these trees were being felled.

You may say it was just that Bernie Kemp

couldn't count – but Bernie has all his wits about him. Able (my husband) put Bernie in charge of the felling, and in our kitchen over a cup of tea, Able said, "Enough firewood, I reckon, out of them eight oak to last a good few winters." "Seven oak," said Bernie, "and two larch." "Eight," said Able, as if Bernie had made a slip of the tongue.

"Counted them this morning," said Bernie, though he sounded puzzled. "There's only seven'm – though yesterday I'd have said you were right, Able. And two larch."

"The upshot was, when Bernie came in that night, he admitted that there were eight oak as Able had said, but insisted that he and his men had counted only seven, though they had checked and double-checked because they all thought that there had been eight earlier, and of course, it doesn't take much checking to be sure of seven great trees instead of eight. One man swore that the tree lying nearest Bosky Wood (when they counted eight) wasn't there when they counted seven.

One of the men helping Bernie was so upset by the next thing that happened, he went home, and didn't come back until his wife nagged him into it (his words, Ma'am). Now, Bernie, who had all his wits about him as I say, is a bit deaf, and maybe that had something to do with the misunderstanding, though how Bernie couldn't hear a chainsaw, I don't know

– but when a tree was felled, this man (the one with the wife) would lop off the branches with his chainsaw. The mound isn't big, Ma'am, covering as much ground as a small house, but with a couple of great trees felled and the rest still standing, the place was full of branches sticking out in all directions, thick with leaves, so you could easily lose sight of a man a few yards off.

Bernie accused the man of not working, because the sound of the saw stopped for minutes on end, but the man said that of course he was working, but the saw wasn't. He said the saw kept cutting out, then switching on again like it had a mind of its own. Well, Bernie examined the saw and could find nothing wrong, but the man vanished among the branches and the sound of the saw stopped. Then the man popped out of nowhere, it seemed, making Bernie jump, and the man was pretty startled too. All this put some ill-feeling between Bernie and his helper, but that disappeared when they agreed that only seven oak were felled – as I already explained to Your Majesty.

Ma'am, there are more stories I could tell you, but this letter is long enough. All I can say is that more and more strange things are happening around Bosky Wood, and I hope you can find someone to help find out what's going on before things come to a head – though what that head might be, I can't imagine. I have asked the police, but there's nothing to show them (or almost nothing, for I do have something that an expert might recognize), and I can't expect the police to act on just my stories.

As I say, Ma'am, I'm getting nervous, and would appreciate some help.

I have the honour to remain, Madam, Your Majesty's most humble and obedient servant.

G. Grimshaw

Grace Grimshaw (Mrs)

CHAPTER ONE

When I wake in the night, it's never dark.

The street lights shine rectangles up onto the ceiling. One rectangle is squint because its window is on the side wall of my bedroom and the light slips in at an angle.

This window looks into the gap between our building and the next. The space between the buildings is just wide enough for Mum's Rolls Royce to scrape through into the garage.

Don't let "Rolls Royce" mislead you. Mum won the stupid thing in a raffle twenty years ago. You've no idea how embarrassing it is stepping out of a Rolls Royce Motor Car. But more of that later.

Our house is over Mum's antique shop, and leans on the house-over-the-grocer's next door, which rests against *et cetera*, all down our bendy little street.

No one glancing up from the pavement would believe the maze of stairs and rooms; the sheer *ancientness* of our house. Queen Elizabeth the First never slept here, but she could have.

Come to think of it, she could pop in today and consider it up to date. The stool I wobble into my tights on is sixteenth century.

I woke slowly.

Sweat rolled off my stomach under my pyjamas.

The rectangles clung to the ceiling.

I closed my eyes.

Thud! I sat up.

"Stella!"

"Daniel?" I heaved out of bed and ran to the side window.

Daniel's face shone in the street light. His arm was up, about to throw another clod of grass. I pulled the window further open and bumped my head (as usual) on the double glazing. I opened the double glazing.

"Let me in! Hurry!"

"Dan-iel!"

"Stella!"

I was ready to argue, but that *Stella!* carried fear, and I fled, jumping down the five steps of the top flight.

The night-light on the landing glowed down into the tunnel of the lower flight. I descended two steps at a time, and hauled back the bolts on the street door.

Before the bang of the lock had died, Daniel was squashed in beside me and turning the key again. I smelt sweat on him, and felt the heat of his body. His shirt stuck to his skin. He retreated to sit, gasping, on the bottom step. "Bolt the door!"

"I don't hear anyone."

It was partly a question; partly reassurance. I wasn't surprised he was sweating. I was sweating. It was the hottest August in years. But Daniel was panting as if he'd run for miles. I bolted the door.

I said: "What are you doing out? It's been dark for hours! What's wrong?"

Night-lights glow on our landings because the staircase has no windows. The lamp in this tiny lobby had Mum's favourite orange bulb, so it was a second before I noticed Daniel's colour. I said, "Daniel, our candles are less waxy looking— "

He leapt at me.

His hand clamped onto my mouth.

Sweat dribbled on his brow.

Then I heard.

God help us, I heard!

I suppose – really – it wasn't much of a noise; just a scrabbling on the pavement, then a scratching on the door.

I tried to push free of Daniel, when I realized

something which made me hesitate.

The scratching was *all over* the door.

For a second, I tried to picture how anyone could scratch all over the door, all at once. I mean, if it was a *person* – the sound would have been here and there, as whoever-it-was scraped with their fingernails.

I just couldn't think how the scratching was being done.

And because I couldn't think how it was being done, I couldn't imagine what was standing on our pavement.

Which was when Daniel's fear sank into me, and I felt, *God-help-us*.

So we stood, Daniel and me, sweating in the little hall, Daniel's palm pressed to my mouth.

The scratching went on.

We could have strolled up the stairs – pretending nothing was wrong.

Or wandered into the shop. The door to the shop was at my back; covered in green baize. We could have looked out the shop window.

We didn't move.

Then the scratching stopped.

We listened.

Something rustled on the pavement.

Then silence.

Daniel eased his palm from my mouth and dabbed his shirt sleeve on his forehead.

His face bent to mine, but I reached for the door and edged it open.

Light from a streetlamp filled the shop window. Furniture in the window buried us in shadow.

I put my mouth to Daniel's ear. "The floorboards creak."

He nodded. He knew that as well as I did.

I crept into the shop, Daniel's fingers on my spine. I remembered that only pyjamas came between me and the night air, and my face bloomed warmly; I mean, Daniel and I had been *that* close!

I paused before stepping into a strip of light which lay along the floor. My first glimpse outside had told me the street was deserted, but I hesitated again.

Despite the heat, a shiver danced on my skin.

I peered around the bulk of a chesterfield in the window.

A dead moth lay in the curve of a displayed Paisley shawl. Across the road, the Bank of England – like a toy Parthenon – sagged as if asleep, and threatened to topple onto the two cars in the little car park next door.

Then –

Y'know how – when something odd is happening – a simple thing can hold your attention?

I thought, *What a dumb place to plant a tree.*

I'd never noticed, but a tree stood between

the cars in the car park, its arms raised in a spindly bundle, the yellow light from the streetlamp shining on the edge of every twiggy branch.

But nothing moved.

I advanced into Mum's window display and looked out the side window at our doorway.

Nothing there, either. And nothing in the further doorway which is the shop door for customers, with a jangling bell.

The elegant little street dozed in the summer night.

"Stella?"

"Follow me," I whispered, and I led Daniel among our antiques, towards the rear of the shop, where a longcase clock clunks away the seconds.

Another lobby leads to the shop's kitchen. From this lobby, the back staircase goes up into the house.

I switched on the kitchen light, and in the light's brightness I saw horror lingering in Daniel's face. I had meant to fill the kettle, but my legs melted, and I plumped onto a chair.

Daniel knelt in front of me, and I held his hands.

I couldn't believe how much I was shaking.

Then my mother leapt in.

My mother leapt into the kitchen.

Above her head, she held an African

18

knobkerrie, which is a club. Swinging the knobkerrie down would have ripped out the ceiling. Swinging it sideways would have swept the cupboards off the wall, then squashed Daniel and me into jelly.

That knobkerrie is made of ironwood. Mr Hilary, the grocer, pottering in our shop one morning at coffee time, casually tried to pick it up. He thought Mum had wired it to the mantelpiece. And Mr Hilary isn't small.

Neither is my mum.

She's six feet one in her slippers and lean as a greyhound – especially inside her silk dressing-gown.

When she leapt into the kitchen, I shrieked. She must've drifted down the back stairs like a ghost. Every board in this house creaks.

"Stella!" she gasped. "What are you doing! What are you both doing!"

Daniel stood up hurriedly. "Sorry, Mrs Lane!"

Mother glared at Daniel as if he had no right being male.

My breath quivered. I must have looked as if I was going to cry. Mother dropped the knobkerrie and tangled me in her embrace.

"You can tell me!" she cooed.

"Mum!" I pushed free.

"Mrs Lane! There was something outside."

Mum looked at Daniel.

"Daniel threw earth at my window," I said.

"I let him in the front door."

"Then that's what woke me. Good thing I took the knobkerrie upstairs. Mrs Roper complained of prowlers. Then I combed my hair—"

A shudder took me by surprise, and Mum stared. Daniel's cheeks still shone like candle wax.

My mother whirled out, then marched in carrying a decanter and glasses on a tray.

"I don't like whisky," whispered Daniel.

"It isn't whisky!" snapped Mother. "It's medicine. Down the hatch! Now!"

We obeyed.

She put the kettle on and rummaged savagely for mugs and coffee. Cold ham appeared, and we gulped the coffee and demolished sandwiches as if we hadn't eaten for a week.

Then Mother tipped herself another whisky and slid the decanter out of reach.

"Now," she said.

I looked at Daniel.

"I saw nothing in the street," said Mother encouragingly. "I looked from the shop window." She tilted her whisky glass towards Daniel. "Why were you out in the middle of the night?"

"Sorry, Mrs Lane."

"That's not an explanation!"

"I'm sorry!"

The desperation in Daniel's voice stopped

her. His eyes slid towards me, but didn't quite reach my face.

"I was with ... Susie Kelso."

I sat, unbelieving.

Susie Kelso.

I jerked my face away. Tears gathered on my lashes.

"It wasn't a date! I met her this afternoon. We just hung around together. We fell asleep—"

"Fell asleep!" I yelped.

"Let him talk—"

"He's been doing more than talking!" I rammed my chair back and ran. I heard another chair scrape, then Mum's voice. I blundered into the shop.

I stood very straight in the darkness, my lips tight to keep them from trembling.

I sucked in a breath.

I gasped, "Who cares!" at the shadows.

Yellow light shone on the chesterfield.

"Who cares," I mumbled.

I wandered into the window display and sprawled on the chesterfield, but the leather was cold through my pyjamas so I sat on the edge of the seat, sniffing.

Where had Daniel gone, that he could fall asleep with Susie Kelso?

If I'd been born dead I would have missed tonight. If I'd been born a tree like the one between the cars in the car park, I would have been more beautiful than Mum.

21

I leaned towards the glass of our shop window.

I knuckled my tears, and stared into the car park. I saw the two cars dozing in the yellow light from the streetlamp. I saw grass sprouting around their tyres. But between the cars, where I had seen the tree with its thin branches, was nothing at all.

Just the night, and silence and – inside me – a great chunk of fear.

CHAPTER TWO

I ran into the kitchen and stopped. I didn't
know what to say. Trees don't disappear.

Mother gazed at me over her whisky.

Daniel said, "Stella—" but I ignored him.

"Come!" I croaked, and Mother came.

Daniel followed. Through the shop.

"Stella?" whispered Mother. Her eyes
moved hugely, full of darkness.

I told her about the tree. She stared from the
shop window.

She said, "There's never been a tree—"

I shrieked in a whisper, "I swear it was
there! Between the cars in the car park! Daniel
saw it!"

Daniel shrugged. He hadn't noticed.

Mother loomed across the yellow light
which flooded the window display. There was
definitely no tree in the bank car park. She

vanished towards the green baize door.

Cooler air drifted into the shop.

Nothing else changed. No sound from the green door. Not even the lock turning in the front door.

But Mother appeared on the pavement.

Her dressing-gown nipped her waist. Her hair flowed as she moved. She had left the knobkerrie in the kitchen, but in her raised fist was the curling stone we use as a doorstop.

A curling stone.

Which weighs eighteen kilos – or about forty pounds.

And my mother was threatening the empty street with it.

Oh, perhaps this isn't the moment, but... Mother was once a model.

People she's never met treat her like a friend whose name they've forgotten; those who've read *Vogue*.

The point is, to keep in shape, Mother pumped iron. Weight training. She still does.

So on the pavement, she held the curling stone high, and marched from our sight.

Daniel and I advanced into the window. Mother popped out from the gap between our building and the next – that is, the lane into our garage – then crossed the road and vanished among the pillars of the bank. She reappeared and strode into the car park. I grabbed Daniel's wrist.

Mother wandered back onto the street and shrugged at us.

She came in, locked the front door, and herded us through to the kitchen. She lugged me onto her knee as if I was eight, and for once, I didn't mind.

"Someone," she demanded, "had better start at the beginning."

Daniel sighed.

I slid off Mum's knee and switched on the kettle. I didn't want to look at Daniel when he mentioned Susie Kelso.

"...cycling in the square," Daniel was saying, "parking her bike. She called, 'Wait for me!' So I waited. She went into the baker's, and I bought a bar of ice-cream and sat on the cathedral wall with my eyes shut against the sun. You could have fried an egg on my face!

"And you know the scruffy lawn between the wall and the cathedral? The cedar trees make it gloomy with their thick branches – even on a day as sunny as this. So much shade! I finished my ice-cream and looked around for a bin.

"I noticed something odd. I still don't know what it means, but Stella – you saw a tree in the car park? Crazy mistake! It's crazy all right! Listen.

"The nearest bin was on the cathedral lawn – beside the path to the cathedral door. No distance away, but... You know the big cedar? The bin's almost under it. Well, I'm as batty as you, Stella. The air seemed filled with thin branches. I know the cedar is thick and droopy, but my impression was of hundreds of twiggy branches.

"I didn't like that, so I avoided the lawn – a few strides would've taken me across it. Instead, I walked into the square and found a bin there. Susie came out of the baker's."

Daniel drank his coffee.

In the shop, the longcase clock chimed three.

Mum asked quietly, "Shouldn't you phone home?"

"Thanks, Mrs Lane. Yes. I phoned earlier, but..." Mum waved him towards the phone beside the knobkerrie.

I didn't listen to his excuses to his mother.

He finished with, "Everything's OK. Yes, she's here." He glanced at Mum. "You know I wouldn't. Stella's my friend. Oh, hold on! She says can I stay over? Thanks, Mrs Lane. That's OK, Mum. I've stayed before! You shouldn't believe what you see on television! 'Night."

He sat at the table. "Sorry about all that."

Mum smiled with her mouth, but her eyes waited.

"Susie," said Daniel, "had bought buns and cans of coke. 'You're not busy,' she said. 'We'll picnic at Bosky Wood.'

"I said, 'You can't get into Bosky Wood. It's

26

solid undergrowth. Even my dad can't remember being in it – and he remembers everything he ever did.'

"'And everything he ever didn't!' She's got a smart mouth, Susie Kelso."

"And boobs," I muttered.

"We cycled out of town. I had forgotten that I'd avoided the cathedral lawn. We were sweating, but she refused to stop for a coke. I reckon it's six miles to Bosky Wood. She complained about her shirt sticking to her skin—"

"I bet *you* didn't!"

"You know how bad-tempered she gets. By the time I'd lifted the bikes over the iron gate into that field at the corner of the wood, she was wishing she'd bought wine instead of coke. She wanted cake instead of buns. And why hadn't I brought anything!

"The field was rutted by tractor wheels, so she threw her bike down and refused to push it further. I chained my bike to hers and we walked to the tree stumps – where they grow out of the mound. It's only a few paces, Mrs Lane.

"She wanted to explore the wood. But a glance showed it was impossible. 'According to my dad,' I reminded her, 'he wasn't allowed near Bosky Wood when he was a boy. Then, when he was old enough to risk it, the shrubbery was too thick to walk through.

27

Maybe it always was.'

"'Well!' said Susie in that smart way of hers, 'somebody should look after the place! I thought woods were valuable! How can the owner just leave it? Some people have no sense!'

"'Dad says the ground's too stony. He remembers being told that. And you know perfectly well that Grimshaw owns the land. Always has done. If the stones are like the one you're sitting on, then even clearing the trees would be a waste of time. The land's useless.'

"She told me to be quiet. I know I go on sometimes, but I like thinking through a problem..."

"What happened then?" demanded Mother.

Daniel looked at me, but I stared at the table top. This was the part he'd skid over. Once the drink and buns are done, and the sun's melting in the sky and larks burbling and Susie Kelso's shirt is sticking to her chest...

"I fell asleep first. Susie was prowling along the fence beside the wood. She said the stones in the mound looked shaped, as if for building. When I woke up, my arm was under her neck. The sun sparkled through the treetops.

"The shadow of Bosky Wood covered the mound – though the air was as hot as an oven. It was eight o'clock. I said I should get home. To tell you the truth, I was embarrassed."

I turned deliberately and stared at Daniel.

"I was," he insisted. "I mean, I didn't mind, but…"

"But she is gorgeous and you couldn't think what to do."

"Stella," said Mother quickly, "would you kindly check that I bolted the front door? Thank you. *Thank* you."

The door was secure – as we knew – but when I sat down again, Daniel had stopped making excuses.

"I told Susie to help gather up our rubbish," he said. "She would have thrown the cans into the wood. 'Nobody goes in anyway!' she sniped. And I said that animals can hurt themselves—"

"Stop preaching!" I snapped. "It's the middle of the night and I want to know where you've been and what you've been doing!" I glared. "Where you've been, anyway."

Daniel huddled into himself. "I've been haunted," he whispered.

His cheeks sat like wax on his bones, and sweat oozed on his temples.

From the shop, I heard the slow *clunk* of the longcase clock.

"We put our rubbish into the carrier bag Susie had brought the buns in. She kept looking round. 'Let's go!' she said. 'I don't like this place!'

"'You liked it all afternoon,' I told her. 'What's the matter?'

29

"Her face burned with heat and sun, but she shivered. She said – she came close, glancing behind her. She said, 'We're being watched.'"

"You know the mound, Stella. Tree stumps and stones in the grass. And behind the fence, the woods struggling to get out. And the iron gate we had climbed over, set in the hedge. No one could be in the wood. She held my arm. 'Something's watching us.'"

"'I don't see anyone,' I said."

"She wasn't pretending. You know – making an excuse to get close. She was scared. I said, 'Even if someone is watching—'"

"'Not a person,' she said."

"'There might be a fox...' But she clung to me. And she was right. It seemed the wood was thicker. I couldn't understand that. Bosky Wood's shadow was cooler, and the trees rustled as if a wind stirred. But no wind moved on our skin."

"So we walked towards the bikes."

Daniel's voice faded. He looked at Mum as if needing her to believe what he was going to say. "Stella," he whispered.

I waited.

"The bikes lay near the iron gate. I'd chained them together, and left them on the tractor tracks."

"Yes?" I whispered.

"There are no trees in the field, Stella."

"Of course not."

"But there was a tree beside the bicycles. I only glimpsed it. Some trick of the light kept me from focussing on it. And I was already panicking. We ran. Not to the gate, because the tree was there. We ran across the pasture, then followed the hedge until we found another gate. We ran away, Stella, along the road. We walked. And jogged. The sun jiggled behind Bosky Wood. We kept walking, and Susie stared at me now and then, but she didn't speak. Though we had both seen... I know it doesn't make sense, but – Mrs Lane? I could've sworn that the tractor tracks ran on either side of the tree.

"Though – as I say – I only had a glimpse."

Daniel steadied his breath.

"It was dark when I got Susie home. She shut the door in my face.

"I suppose I could have gone home too. But ... some things can't wait. Bosky Wood is creepy enough even in sunlight; had we fooled ourselves about that tree? Susie hadn't mentioned it. She'd said almost nothing on the way back to town. Maybe she thought I was crazy making her run away, and that's why she kept looking at me. But I remembered she had glanced around before we left the mound, and held onto me because she felt that something was watching.

"I was too tired to think. I phoned Mum, told her I'd left my bike and was taking the last bus out of town. I would cycle home.

"The bus turns off before Bosky Wood.

"After the brightness inside the bus, the landscape seemed heaped with darkness. I walked quickly under the starlight. A skull nodded beside a tree, and my heart turned over, but the skull was a cow scratching its jaw on the tree's bark.

"At last the beginning of the hedge was at my hand. Behind the hedge lay the pasture that Susie and I had fled through. And there was the gate we'd climbed to reach the road. Should I climb it again and cross the pasture? Or stay on the road until I got to the iron gate? The bicycles were only a few paces into the field.

"I preferred the road. In my pocket, I found the key for the padlock that held Susie's bike chained to mine. I strode on through the warm night.

"Bosky Wood rose behind the hedge, and I stopped, standing silently on the tarmac.

"Stars filled the sky. Surely, I thought, only the pasture is behind the hedge? (Because I hadn't yet reached the iron gate.)

"Starlight can make you see things. As I walked along the road, shrubs became men, so maybe rising ground, thick with grass, can become a forest. I stared at the trees beyond the hedge.

"Their spindly shapes crowded the sky, and

32

their branches tapped, like whispering. And I hesitated.

"If the trees were really there, I told myself, then I had passed the iron gate. But I knew I hadn't passed the gate.

"And growing on me was that feeling of being watched. I walked along the far side of the road from the pasture.

"Then I came to a tree half in the hedge which protected me from the pasture, its roots tangling like rope onto the tarmac. I shivered. I couldn't recall Susie or me bumping over these roots on our bikes when we went for our picnic.

"I walked on, conscious of the branches tapping. But I had come for the bikes, and the bikes I would get.

"I reached the iron gate and looked over. I saw the tractor ruts like black slashes in the earth. I saw the gleam of the bicycles. There was no tree between the tracks. There were no trees filling the pasture.

"Maybe I had dreamt them.

"The key for the chain was clamped in my fist. I climbed the gate and ran to the bikes. It took seconds to find the padlock. More seconds to jiggle the key into the keyhole. The click of the lock startled me. I dragged the chain free, and raised my bike onto its wheels. I carried it, running, to the gate and dumped it over onto the grass verge. One more dash for

Susie's bike and I'd be burning rubber.

"Stella.

"Stella, can you imagine being alone six miles outside of town? in the starlight? and not knowing if those tapping things would show up? When I turned from the gate to fetch Susie's bike, oh, Stella! oh, God! *something touched me!*

"I don't remember climbing the gate," whispered Daniel. "I was running back along the road. I didn't dare pause even to grab my bike. My flesh quivered like cold jelly. I don't know why I was so horrified, but I was. I heard myself moaning, and managed to stop that. I ran the six miles to town."

"Then the streetlamps of the Westgate shone on the pavement, and for the first time, I slowed. Then I sprawled in a shop doorway, my lungs torn for want of breath. I was soaked in sweat. My legs shook. I wondered if I'd be able to stand up again, but not for a second did I stop looking along the Westgate. Not for a moment, Stella, did I stop straining to see the way I had come, striving to hear.

"What would I do if the tapping things followed me? That made me think. I'd never make it home. You were nearest, Stella. If I had to run again, I would run here.

"You know Sloane's the Butcher in the Westgate? You know! the half-timbered shop, where the Labrador sleeps in the doorway and customers have to step over him? That's right. The council built a garden on that corner. With conifers. For a second I thought the conifers had grown.

"I held my breath. But my chest struggled for air. I panted.

"Then a clattering – like a thousand twigs tapping – whispered down the lane, and I fled again.

"I dodged along the alleys between the Westgate and here. I think I did lose them for a minute – whatever they were. Long enough to find clumps of grass in the bank car park and throw them at your window. Thanks for letting me in so quickly, Stella.

"If they'd touched me again, I think I would have died."

CHAPTER THREE

Bacon woke me. Its smell walked around on my taste buds.

Daylight had wiped away the night.

I found Daniel in my kitchen.

My kitchen is across the landing from my bedroom.

Down the five steps of the top flight is a bathroom and Mum's kitchen, which is *the* kitchen for the house.

Last night Daniel had talked in the shop kitchen on the ground floor. And there is a fourth kitchen in the self-contained flat under the rafters. (Where Daniel sleeps when he stays.) Mum lets this to holiday-makers for hundreds of pounds a week.

Sorry. I'm sure nobody cares if the house is stuffed with kitchens. Daniel was stirring bacon in my frying pan.

"Put something on," said Daniel, so I retreated, feeling near-to-naked in pyjamas in the daylight. So I hopped into what Mum calls my clown outfit. She chose it, with my approval. It's cool for this weather, and doesn't expose me to the sun. I'm a redhead like Mum, with white skin that enjoys freckles. Mum used to tell me not to mind my freckles. "You are beautiful," she assured me. I don't know why she bothered. One look in a mirror told me I was beautiful. And my freckles made me different from ordinary folk with their all-over skin colour. Sorry, again. Though I must say that I'm not conceited. It's the way God made me – with the help of cosmetics for special dates. Where was I?

I hauled on my clown outfit. Blue and white striped cotton dungarees, and a puffy-shouldered blouse. Practical – with white and pink trainers to round it off. And I was already washed, having showered before going to bed at three in the morning. Or thereabouts. I brushed my hair until it bounced in curls, then returned to the bacon.

"Did you pinch the grub from Mum's kitchen?"

"I'm cooking this by royal command." Daniel glanced at me. He turned down the gas. Glanced again.

"What?" I asked.

"How can you look like that in just sixty

seconds? My mum takes an hour to look ordinary."

I smiled.

Daniel didn't. He stared at me.

"The bacon's scorching," I said, and whatever Daniel was contemplating saying died on his lips. He forked the bacon onto its raw side, and cracked eggs into the pan, picking out bits of shell with quick fingers.

"I usually have tea and toast," I told him. He smiled and said the kettle had boiled.

We ate, foreheads almost touching over the tiny eighteenth-century table. More than once, Daniel opened his mouth to speak, but always put bacon or egg in. I wanted him to say nothing. Things between us were fine. I'd forgiven him for Susie Kelso.

"You're wearing my shirt!" I accused him.

"Your mum borrowed it for me. It's a good length. I needed a bath, and my shirt was whiffy with sweat. You don't mind?"

"As long as she didn't lend you my pants."

Daniel laughed. He laughed well. He reminded me of my father.

He said, "Have you looked out of the window this morning?"

My stomach pushed food back up.

"Don't worry!" he cried. "There's nothing there that shouldn't be. I only asked."

"Oh! My heart! I'll make the tea! I need it to wash down my bacon! Are you sure? Were

38

you out? I never thought."

"There's nothing."

"We should visit Susie."

He stared.

"I want to know," I said, "what she saw in the pasture. We can't leave it."

Daniel turned to the toaster and dropped in bread. He lifted away my eggy plate. He served marmalade. Then stood at the kitchen window, his legs brown and lean. The kitchen window overlooks the garage and the back garden. "Nothing in the garden," he sighed. The toast popped up.

So we crunched and drank tea.

Once he dipped his spoon into the marmalade and left it, and touched my hair. Then he marmaladed toast and we crunched again.

"We could fetch the bikes," he mumbled.

I think he hoped I'd say no. I said, "Good idea. Is Mum in the shop?"

"Huh! Hours ago!"

"Nice day."

"Stella—"

"You wash up!" I said brightly. "I'll clean my teeth!" And I fled down the five steps to the bathroom and gave Daniel time to tidy my kitchen. Some words are best not said.

The bus left us.

I watched its wheels churning dust from the grass verge.

The nearest house was a tan smudge three fields away, leaking a thread of smoke.

Daniel said, "It's a hot day for hunting monsters." The sky blinded me. "That was supposed to be funny."

"I don't think I could run six miles," I said. I recalled the scratching on the front door, and shivered. Daniel touched my arm, encouraging me along the road to Bosky Wood.

The wood looked as I remembered it. Shrubs stretched through the fence into the pasture, like prisoners reaching for freedom. Daniel's bike leaned on this side of the iron gate. Susie's lay on the tractor tracks. There was no tree. The pasture curved grassy-bright under the sun.

Daniel climbed over the gate. He returned with Susie's bike and climbed the gate again. His smile said *Nothing to it*.

"So far," I agreed and he grinned, recognizing that I had understood.

Bosky Wood stood frozen in the heat, green as a hillside. I looked behind me. Across the road, fields shimmered with corn. The tan farmhouse poured smoke. I sat astride Susie's bike. The saddle was too low. I adjusted it, and looked again at the farmhouse.

Smoke burst from the front of the house. The *boom!* of an explosion reached us – hot air blowing a window out.

We wasted two seconds, gaping. Then:

"Move, Stella!" Daniel was running with his bicycle, following the road beside the wood. By the time I had mounted, he was cycling furiously.

I stood on the pedals. No cars moved between the hedges which bordered the tarmac.

Daniel skidded into the farm track on the opposite side of the road from the wood, and we bounced along beside the corn fields.

The house was flat-fronted with brown stone walls. Georgian, I told myself, categorizing it for when I told Mum. At least five rooms to the front.

We threw the bikes down. Smoke from a first floor window had already rolled across the field. Fire roared inside the house.

"What do we do!" I screamed.

"Round the back! There may be a door open!"

We ran. A barn stood separate behind the house, plus a garage and smaller buildings.

"See if there's a hose!" yelled Daniel. He raced towards the house. I ran to the barn. I heard a crash, and turned. Daniel was swinging a shovel through a window. He scraped away the last of the glass. "Get a move on, Stella!" He clambered into the house, and I saw him glance around. Then he moved out of sight.

The barn offered me nothing but bales of hay. I ran back into the yard. A tap sprouted beside the garage. The garage was locked. I bobbed up to see in the window. A Volvo glittered dimly. If the car was there, then somebody was at home – in the burning house. But the tap meant there was probably a hose for washing the car. And the hose would be in the garage.

I tugged the garage padlock. I needed a lever. This had to be the tidiest farmyard in the county!

I ran to the smashed window and lifted the shovel. I fled back to the garage and swung viciously at the padlock. The blows almost broke my fingers. If the edge of the shovel would hit the padlock on its top surface, it might loosen the hasp. I thought of my mother wielding the knobkerrie. If she can do it…! I brought the shovel down on target.

The padlock flopped open. In a moment I was hauling the door wide, filling the garage with daylight.

The hose hung on a hook. A minute passed while I fastened the hose to the tap and turned on the water. I grabbed the nozzle and ran, the hose leaping behind me. But it didn't reach the house.

I screamed in through the window. "Daniel! Daniel! The hose isn't long enough! Where are you!" I dropped the hose, leaving it to water the yard, and climbed over the windowsill into the room. I opened a door and stood in the hall. A staircase rose into smoke. "Daniel!" I gasped.

Smoke, I knew, could kill in seconds. Then I was up the stairs and choking on the landing. The smoke oozed in around a door facing me.

"Daniel!" I screamed; and coughed. Then I remembered what the fireman visiting our school had said, and crawled, my face at the floor.

I reached up to the nearest door handle – beside the door that was smoking. I turned the handle and crawled in fast, shutting the door behind me. The air was fresh. But empty of Daniel.

I darted to the window and glimpsed the hose still wriggling water onto the yard.

Opposite the window a second door stood shut and I wondered if it led into the burning room. I hesitated. Opening that door even a finger's breadth could blast fire in on me.

But Daniel might be behind it.

I ran and jerked the door open, then immediately slammed it shut. Only smoke puffed in.

I hauled the front of my blouse out of my dungarees and stuffed a bunch of it over my face.

I opened the door again, and crawled under the smoke. Fire roared.

Flames raged dimly at the far side of the room. I glimpsed another door, and guessed that it led to the room that was leaking smoke onto the landing – the same room where hot air had burst the window outwards. Heat curled my eyebrows. Water ran from my eyes. All I could see, now, was a polished timber floor under my nose, the edge of a rug – and a hand.

The hand was Daniel's. I grabbed it and the fingers moved. I gripped his wrist, took a breath, stood up and hauled. He should have slid on that polished floor, but he might have been nailed down. I dropped, and crawled beside his arm to his head. His head was gone, encased in his shirt. "Good thinking!" I gasped. And he shook free and pointed towards his feet.

I hauled myself along his leg as far as the knee. The rest of his leg was buried under a gigantic bundle of clothes. His other leg pushed at the bundle. I wondered why he was unable to move a load of old clothes. When I grabbed the bundle I found out. It was full of flesh. I touched a woman's bare arm, limp, and heavy as wet cement. I heaved, trying to move her. Eyes streaming, I strained. If Mum had been here she'd have thrown this human elephant aside as if it weighed forty kilos.

"Push!" I gasped. Daniel pushed with his foot and I used my shoulder. Daniel tore his leg from under the bundle and we crawled desperately into the room with fresh air.

We sprawled, coughing. Daniel's face and

clothes were dark with smoke. "We've got to get her out!" he groaned.

"Have you phoned the fire brigade!" I yelled.

"People out first!" he gasped. "Ready?"

"We'll never move her!"

"She's half on a rug! You pull! I'll push!" And we dived into the burning room.

I knew instantly why Daniel had said that I should pull and he should push – not so far for me to go into the room. He had to scramble over the body, vanishing into coiling smoke. He must have put his feet against something, for when I pulled the rug, the huge flopping bundle shifted. The nearer we got to the door, the harder I had to pull; Daniel had lost purchase with his feet. I thought of my mother and her iron muscles. I kicked the door wide and pretended I was Super Stella. The polished floor continued into the other room, and the woman slid through. Daniel wasn't pushing. I got behind the mountain of flesh and shoved it clear of the door. I dived into the smoke and hauled Daniel out. I shut the door. Smoke filled this room now. Desperation gave me energy. I hurled a coffee table through a window.

The smoke writhed away.

Daniel, on his hands and knees, coughed until I thought his lungs would appear. Then: "Help me!" And we humped the woman face-down and Daniel pumped her ribs to force breath into her. "Phone's in the hall!" he gasped, and I ran, down the stairs, wiping my eyes, choking, and phoned the fire brigade.

A thick haze filled the staircase. I held my breath and ran up through the haze and into the room. Fresh air sucked smoke out through the broken window.

"She's breathing!" panted Daniel.

"The fire brigade'll be seven minutes!"

We looked at smoke pouring in around the door from the burning room.

"We must get her out!" coughed Daniel.

"She's a whale!"

"Slide her to the landing!"

"The landing's unbreathable!" I shrieked. "If she sticks there, she'll suffocate! Shouldn't we get her to the window? At least there's air, and the firemen can reach her!"

"They couldn't lift her! Help me stuff something under this door." We grabbed cushions and crushed them close to the door with an armchair.

"We must slow the fire down!" gasped Daniel. "Didn't you find a hose?"

"It wouldn't reach."

We turned the woman face-up and dragged her by the arms. We pushed furniture aside until her head lay under the window. Her bosom, inside a green apron, heaved like Bosky Wood in a gale. Smoke streamed in despite our cushions, and fled away into the sunshine. "There must be a bathroom," said Daniel.

He saw my look. "For water, Stella! If we bring the hose up—"

I ran, holding my breath again, squeezing my eyes near-shut as I crossed the landing, past the door that leaked smoke – opened another door on the landing, and saw an iron bath. Thirty seconds later I was pushing the hose onto the cold tap and screwing the fixture tight. I turned on the water. The hose squirmed. By now, coughing seemed as natural as breathing. Smoke layered the air. I scurried face-to-the-floor across the landing, the hose jetting water.

I stopped at the door that leaked smoke. Fire roared somewhere behind it. I dared not open it. I jammed the nozzle at the gap underneath. But the gap was too narrow. Half the jet sprayed back off the door's surface. I tore the nozzle from the hose and squeezed the bare end under. I knew that the amount of water flooding through was too little. Bangs blasted, as objects shattered in the heat. Roasting air stung my lungs.

I retreated into the fresher air beside Daniel. He had pushed an armchair to the window and was struggling to raise the woman into it. Smoke still spewed in around the cushions at the door. More smoke followed me from the landing. "The fire brigade should be soon!"

I gasped. "What are you doing?"

"Every second could count! I've jammed the window open and cleared the broken glass." I stared out at the table I'd thrown through the window. "If we get her onto this armchair," said Daniel, "we may be able to drape her over the sill. I hope they bring a strong fireman! What have you done with the hose? I saw you crossing the yard to undo it from the tap. Huh! And I thought your mother could move!"

"There's water spraying into the room where the fire started. From the bathroom. Oh, listen!"

"The fire brigade! Help me lift her!"

CHAPTER FOUR

We didn't have to lift the woman. In two minutes Daniel and I were down a ladder and coughing fresh air. Then the back door of the farmhouse opened, and she emerged wobbling on the firemen's stretcher, her face alien under an oxygen mask. An ambulance brayed up the track and the stretcher was shovelled in.

We wanted to watch the fire-fighters, but though hoses squirted, and steam spumed among the smoke, we were bundled into the ambulance too, and hee-hawed towards town.

When we looked at each other we knew why we were in the ambulance. Our clothes were stiff with soot. We stank of burning. Daniel's hair stuck up, shrivelled like wire wool. His face smiled like a side of half-cooked beef.

"Well done, Stella. But keep away from

mirrors." He coughed, and pointed at my bare arms.

Under the dirt, my skin shone like boiled lobster. Pain dawned on me, and suddenly I didn't dare move.

"My face!" I gasped.

"Seen it better," grinned Daniel, and he touched my hair.

Kind words from the ambulance men (who were busy with the woman) calmed me. I'm not conceited, but burns on my face – !

Relief was complete when a doctor at the hospital assured me the burns were superficial. I won't bore you with lights probing our eyes and lotions cooling our skin; and meeting an anxious Mr Grimshaw (it was Mrs Grimshaw we'd rescued); and hanging around until Mum exploded down the corridor, shrieking at the sight of us; commandeering the matron's phone to make a hair appointment for me. And Daniel's mother's bustling along, humble as a brush salesman, weeping suddenly, but smiling because we were allowed home – at last – then beaming (Daniel's mum, I mean), sweeping through town in our Rolls Royce, her hand raised ready to wave to the crowd. It doesn't seem to matter to Daniel's mum that our Rolls was a prize in a raffle. Fifty quid for a ticket at an antiques fair Charity Event; that's all it cost.

Anyway.

How Daniel slept that night, I don't know, but I hit the mattress after tea, and didn't stir until sunlight whitened my eyelids. And if anything had fumbled along the pavement in the dark hours – well...

Daniel arrived and clumped up to my bedroom as I dropped my ruined clown outfit into a bin bag.

His skin shone, redly tanned, tight across his bones.

"You're not as bad as me, Stella," he said, coming nearly within kissing distance, then holding my hands to look at my arms.

"I close my eyes at mirrors," I told him. "If my skin suffered the same as my clothes..." I unlatched his fingers and heaved the bin bag out the door. "My hair appointment's in half an hour."

"I've been to the hospital."

"Are you all right!"

"To see Mrs Grimshaw. Our whale lady."

"Oh."

I'm always amazed at Daniel's consideration. *My* only thought was that if Mrs Grimshaw had been thinner, we wouldn't have been so burned. "Oh, I never even phoned! How is she?"

"Worried," said Daniel, "about her house." He shook his head. "And something else." He put his hand into his jeans pocket. "When I found her – in that smoke-filled room – she was gasping in a chair. She couldn't move on her own, and I couldn't slide the chair with her in it. She tried to walk. That's when she fell on my leg. Before she passed out she fumbled in her apron pocket and shoved this into my hand."

Daniel placed a wooden tube on my dressing table.

We looked at it.

What was so important about a Victorian pencil case?

I lifted the tube. It was longer than my hand, crudely turned from a knotty bit of fruit wood, and the join in the middle fitted inaccurately.

"Do you know what it is?" asked Daniel.

I told him. "Though," I said, "it's a bit short for pencils. Anything in it?" I put strangling hands around it.

"Don't – "

But the tube opened and twigs spilled onto my dressing table. I squealed, then punched Daniel on the shoulder.

"They're only twigs," he said.

"Then why did you say 'don't'!" I raised my fist again, but he stepped close and hauled my mouth against his.

Confusion.

The twigs had scared me, though I didn't know why. Daniel had been my friend since we met in primary school. I wanted to push him away. But his mouth was warm, and my nerves sighed into the warmth, and his shoulders were thick under my fingers.

I eased my weight onto his toe.

"Stella!"

I turned to the tube and lifted it. "Why did you say 'don't'? They're only twigs."

"Stella…"

"Aren't they?"

"Stella—"

"Oh, shut up! Don't try to change things!"

I stared inside the top end of the tube.

It was a minute before I saw what my eyes were looking at.

"It's not a pencil case," I said. "The end inside would be dotted with lead. It's clean. A kid's box for odds and ends."

Daniel shuffled.

Mother's voice soared up the staircase.

"Daniel," I said, "don't look so anxious!" I hugged him quickly. "I've got to get to the hairdresser's. Meet me in the square at two o'clock. We'll visit Susie Kelso."

"What for? Oh, to tell her that her bike's at Grimshaw's."

We left without touching the twigs.

I want to stay beautiful.

So a wide-brimmed hat kept the sun off my scorched face; air cooled my neck. I regretted my curls being shorn away by the hairdresser, but I decided to enjoy the change. My hair hugged my skull like red feathers.

Mr Hilary was sharing an after-lunch coffee with Mum in the shop kitchen.

"Let's see it!" said Mum, wide-eyed for my hair.

I swept off the hat and posed.

Mum's professional glance measured my head; but I didn't have to wait for *her* approval. Mr Hilary's mouth sagged, and he said, "Well!"

I beamed.

Mother nodded, and dropped a look on Mr Hilary.

We both laughed when Mr Hilary gaped at Mother, then at me, as if he didn't know which feast was the tastier.

He said, "Well!" again, then laughed with us.

"Elaine," he said to Mum. "Watch out for that girl."

"Stella's quite sensible," said Mother.

"Lot of folk aren't," said Mr Hilary. "Don't you stay out late," he told me. "I'm serious. Mrs Roper reckoned she heard prowlers the other night."

"I've a good right hook," I said.

"So've a lot of men. Well, I'd better go. Daisy doesn't like taking charge too long. Terrified of the bacon slicer, she is."

He left, and we heard the bell on the shop door jangle. He reappeared. "A customer," he informed Mum. He whispered to me, "I'd send my Daisy out fire-fighting if she'd come back looking like you."

"Remember to eat," Mum told me, and fingered Mr Hilary away. Daisy is Mr Hilary's daughter. She is not good-looking.

I heard the shop bell jangle again while I unearthed tuna and salad from the fridge.

A laugh from the shop stopped me in mid bite. Mother seldom rose above a chuckle. I stuffed down a mouthful of tomato and wandered through.

Mum often propped her hips on a table when facing male customers. "To prevent them feeling small," she explained. But today's customer stood taller than Mum by a hand's breadth. She laughed again at his remarks and actually touched his arm before she noticed me. Mother is not a flirt.

"Oh, Stella. This is Mr Railford. He's taking the flat for a few days."

He smiled, and raised his eyebrows.

That smile spread a glow down to my toes.

I looked at the floor and gulped tomato.

Mum said, "Mr Railford was to stay at Grimshaw's farm, but—"

"I heard about the fire," he said. "I passed the ambulance on my way to the farmhouse. Your mother says you were in the ambulance?"

I nodded.

He said, "With Mrs Grimshaw? And ... Daniel? Is that right?"

I stared.

His smile widened. He rubbed his hair with one finger, as if embarrassed at knowing so much. A ruffle of hair was left standing, dark as charcoal, and I wanted to press it flat.

"I was coming to work at the farm," explained Mr Railford. "I went to the hospital this morning, and they let me speak to Mrs Grimshaw for a few minutes; then your mother filled in the details about the fire. I spent last night in a hotel, but it's rather public. I specialize in…" He smiled again, melting my knees. "Or rather, I investigate things. And Mrs Grimshaw mentioned your flat – which is particularly convenient." He added. "She's very grateful for what you did."

"Oh." I felt my face warming, remembering that I'd blamed Mrs Grimshaw for being heavy.

"You don't mind my staying here?"

"No."

"Oh, good." He turned to Mother. "My things are in the car. Could I…?"

"Of course. And park in the bank car park. I'll tell them you're staying with us. The manager doesn't mind, so long as you don't use his space."

"Thank you very much."

I retreated into the kitchen. I wondered

what Mr Railford was specially investigating at Grimshaw's farm – and why staying in our house was particularly convenient. He did say that.

I went upstairs to brave a mirror in privacy.

In the hairdresser's I'd glimpsed myself on and off for an hour – now I wanted to know why men raised their eyebrows...

But – enough!

The twigs on my dressing table dared me to pick them up. I didn't touch them. Some ends had broken off, or perhaps had broken off long ago; and bits had collapsed into dust. Which I thought was odd.

But I wasn't really interested.

Downstairs, the longcase clock chimed two. I wiggled into shorts, and spread bronzing lotion up my legs. I chose a long-sleeved shirt to protect my nippy arms and pulled on the hat.

Outside, the sun baked the pavements.

I ran along our little street; I hurried in the shade of the high wall of the cathedral grounds, until I was in the square; and Daniel was waiting – hesitantly.

"What's wrong?"

The cathedral clock chimed two in its tinny old voice – late as usual.

Normally I wouldn't notice the clock, but the chimes emphasized Daniel's hesitation, as if he was waiting for silence.

"It's you," he said.

"What about me?"

He shrugged.

"Are my legs streaky? My face isn't too red? Why aren't you wearing a hat? Your skin must be burning. We'll walk in the shade. Tell me what's wrong."

He crossed the square with me. "Nothing."

"Tell me!" I tried to see my reflection in a shop window.

"You look great," he mumbled.

A man stared at me and I smiled. He smiled, and I took Daniel's arm.

"Ste-lla!"

"What?"

He eased his arm free. "People are looking."

"It's my haircut! I forgot to show you!" I hauled off my hat.

He looked, nodded, and stared at the pavement the way I'd stared at the floor when Mr Railford spoke.

But I didn't understand.

"Is it about Susie Kelso?"

"No. It's just… I can't say it."

"Do you want to see her alone?"

"Who? No, no. Stella, leave it. It's just me."

Daniel managed a dull little smile, which I caught. He let me take his arm for a second, but I stopped at Jenner's to stand on my head to see a price ticket on a jacket, and he strode on.

By the time we reached Susie's door we were chatting normally.

CHAPTER FIVE

Susie stared at us from two steps up. She looked at Daniel's jeans. She looked at me all over.

"Where's my bike?" she demanded.

"Well…" said Daniel.

"You'd better come through." She strode down the little hall. Her shorts were indecently tight. We followed her into a kitchen and out onto a lawn. Susie heaved her hair back and sat on a tartan rug.

"Sit down if you want."

"We won't wait," I said. Susie's glance landed again on Daniel's jeans.

"His legs are scorched," I said.

"Oh." She tilted her face to the sun.

"In a fire."

"A fire?" She stared at my head.

"My hair got burned."

"It's nice. Where's my bike?"

"Aren't you interested in the fire?"

"Not much. You two aren't hurt. I just want my bike. It better not be burnt!"

"Don't worry! Though a fire engine may have flattened it. Aren't you curious? We were nearly killed! Mrs Grimshaw's in hospital—"

"Stella," said Daniel.

I glared at Susie with her legs sprawled to the sun and her shirt full of boobs.

"Your bike's OK," said Daniel. "It's at Grimshaw's farm. We'll fetch it later. Susie, tell us what you saw at Bosky Wood."

Susie gathered her knees within her arms. She scowled at the lawn.

She said, "Nothing much." Her shoulders twitched. "Just..."

She hugged her knees. "Oh! Trees! You know! And the dusk. And *you* ran. So I ran. With that horrible feeling of being watched." She picked grass out of the lawn. "Nothing much."

I said, "You walked six miles."

"I suppose we did."

"You left your precious bike!"

Her glance sprang at me, then she frowned, and rocked like a child, her hair hiding her face.

"I don't know what I saw!" she whispered. "It's as if I'd seen, you know – The Place Between!"

She gazed up at me.

Fear in her eyes stopped my question.

Daniel said, "What do you mean?"

"Don't you know? Don't you know The Place Between? That's what I call it. Hardly anybody knows it. But I've always known. In the darkness, there is *somewhere else* that comes between me and this world.

"When I was tiny I lay in bed and saw that the shadows in my room had other shadows inside them – outlines of other things.

"The more I looked the clearer these outlines became. Grass and hills were between my bed and the curtains – as if our house had crumbled away – as if streets and buildings had disintegrated, leaving the landscape beneath, for me to see.

"Were you at the school camp, oh, in primary seven? Near Cromer? You know – on the Norfolk coast? It was evening, and the teacher took us for a walk along the beach.

"The sky was pale above the sea, and waves rolled onto the sand. The noise of the waves frightened me – to think of that sound rushing and rushing since the beginning of the world.

"I found a horse's skull. I crouched to look at it, and the rest of the kids walked on. When I looked up, I thought something had come out of the sea. I thought a forest of giant crabs with thin arms were thronging the sand, their limbs clattering faintly behind the sea's noise.

But they weren't coming out of the sea. They simply were there.

"I was looking at The Place Between. I think I saw it because of the light, and perhaps my mood. Maybe I imagined it. Maybe I imagined it again at Bosky Wood for it was the same things that I saw – crabs or trees – I don't know. But I was afraid at Bosky Wood because these things don't belong in this world."

She stood up. "What I saw at the wood was real. You tell her," she said to Daniel. "You saw the tree between the tractor's tyre marks!" She turned on me. "And you're right! I didn't walk six miles and leave my precious bike for nothing! You weren't there! You weren't out in the dark with things watching and whispering! Well, I was! And I was terrified!" She strode to the far side of the lawn and stopped, flat-backed, her legs brown below her white shorts.

I think she was crying.

"Come on," said Daniel. "Susie? See you later."

She didn't answer.

We went through the house by ourselves and shut the outside door carefully.

My feelings about Susie Kelso had changed. I'd never thought of her crying. And she knew about The Place Between. I'd never heard of it. It was like discovering that the thickest kid in the town could speak ten languages.

And I no longer envied her those legs. I moved my head, enjoying the summer air around my neck, and thought of Mr Hilary's face when he'd looked at me. Some parts of growing up were good.

"I suppose," said Daniel, "we should fetch Susie's bike."

So we waited at the bus stop in the square. Daniel was quiet. I allowed him to think, while I enjoyed the sun, and men's glances. "Here's the bus."

We trundled free of the town, shaken together on the cool leather seat. Daniel tried to keep six inches of petrol-scented air between us, but the bus did him the favour of bouncing him against me. He was silent until we got to the stop nearest Grimshaw's farm. I didn't listen to his silence. That reminded me of my father too – besides Daniel's laugh, I mean.

The bus groaned away, leaving us in a swirl of dust.

The farmhouse was no longer a brown smudge, but a dirty mark on the countryside.

We walked.

We stared over the hedge at the pasture beside Bosky Wood.

We paused at the iron gate, but the tractor tracks faded distantly into the grass with no spooky tree sprouting between them. We avoided the wood by keeping to the far side of the road.

Then we turned into the lane and approached the farmhouse.

The smell of burning floated in the air; and men's voices. And hammering.

I felt sorry for Mrs Grimshaw and her husband. The middle upstairs window no longer existed. A whole section of wall had dropped onto the gravel in front of the house. Blackened timbers had been added to this pile. I took Daniel's hand.

"Might as well." Mr Grimshaw's voice. The skeleton of an armchair fell from the gap and crashed onto the rubble.

"Hello!" I called.

Mr Grimshaw and another man appeared in the gap. "I'll come down. Round the back. Carry on, will you, Bernie?" The farmer vanished into the ruins. The other man tipped his head at us, and shrugged.

Mr Grimshaw came swiftly, fat, anxious, looking at his black palms, not trying to smile. "Well! You two! How are you? Not so bad? That's grand. Grand. Missus is going to be all right. Thanks to you. I can't never repay you. Never. Look at my house. And your faces. That's not just the sun? 'Course not." He peered up at me, then at Daniel, then at me. "You really are all right? Skin's tighter than a pig's—Sorry.

"I've forgot your names. Stella? Daniel. Good names. Sorry I forgot. Yesterday wasn't the best of days. Look, come through to the kitchen. It's time I had a mug of tea. And Bernie's alus thirsty. You'll take a drink? Blistering sun! Have to use the back door. Got timbers blocking the front hall, shoring up the floor above."

We followed him into the back hall. The staircase was thick with soot and dripping still, with water. The door I had shoved the hose under stood open, its top corner burnt off, and I could see the sky where the roof had fallen in. Rubble spewed onto the landing.

"This way," sighed Mr Grimshaw.

We didn't go upstairs. We stepped over a rolled-up carpet, then into a kitchen. The kitchen was bright and clean except for sooty feathers around the door frame.

"At least we can eat," grunted the farmer. "Got our own generator as a back-up. So the cooker works, and the hot water. I'm glad the missus can't see this. I never been so dirty."

He filled a bucket in the sink and lathered his hands.

"Can we help?" asked Daniel.

"Ur. Mugs in that cupboard. You don't mind a mug, do you?" he asked me.

"No."

"What was you two doing out here yesterday anyway? On a picnic? Blistering sun! I suppose I'm lucky. As Bernie says, that whole field of corn could've caught alight. Water's in the kettle, Stella. Picnic, was it?"

"No," said Daniel. He turned to me.

"No," I said. "We were just looking."

The farmer emptied the bucket and rinsed his hands. "Not much to look at. Unless you're an artist. Got no time for that myself. Folk got to eat, I say. Staring at pictures never fed anybody. Now where's that towel? Though we get one or two every summer setting up easels. Last chap painted Bosky Wood. Wanted me to buy his pictures. Even the missus wouldn't have them, they wur that bad! Ha! Ha! Then off he went in a right old huff. Left some stuff, he went so quick. Out on the pasture. Easel. Paints. Few canvases. Either of you two interested in painting? You could have 'is things. Missus made me put them in the barn. Though he never came back."

"I paint," I said. "If you're sure it's all right."

"All right? Stella, as far as I'm concerned, anything is all right. You saved my missus. There's not enough in this world that I can give you. Both of you. So help yourself when you're ready."

He trudged to the door. "BERNIE! TEA!" He clumped to a stool and accepted a mug. "I need this. Then I'll get on. I want the worst out of the way before the missus comes back. Break her heart, this would."

I said, "Yes."

Then I thought of Mrs Grimshaw unconscious on the floor of the burning room, and I remembered she had given Daniel the wooden tube.

"Daniel," I said, "ask Mr Grimshaw about that pencil case."

"Pencil case?" grunted the farmer.

"Your wife had it in her apron pocket," explained Daniel. "She gave it to me before she passed out. She seemed to think it was important."

"Pencil case," said the farmer again.

"It's really a tube," I said. "Made of fruit wood. It's Victorian, I think—"

"Ha! I know that old thing. 'Twere never a pencil case. Just something my grandfather turned out when he was a boy. Poor job he made of it, too! It's been in this house all its life, if you know what I mean. I don't think anybody used it for anything. Though my missus liked it. Apple wood, she said it was. I dunno. She kept it in a drawer and looked at it once in a blue moon. She said she liked the feel of it, and the colour. Artistic, she is.

"Ah," said Mr Grimshaw, as Bernie appeared in the doorway. "Come on in!" said the farmer loudly. "Shy, is our Bernie. He's been in this kitchen near as often as I have, and he still waits to be asked. Help yourself to tea, Bernie. This is Stella…"

Bernie nodded.

"...and Daniel. You're not brother and sister?"

"Just friends," I said. Daniel stared into his mug.

"Ur." Bernie drank his tea without washing his hands.

Daniel continued staring into his mug with his eyebrows raised. I opened my mouth to speak, but couldn't think of anything.

Mr Grimshaw said, "I wonder what my Grace was a-doing? Why would she give that wooden tube to you, Daniel?" He still spoke loudly, directing his voice at Bernie. Bernie's head jerked as if trying to catch the words in his right ear.

Daniel's eyebrows relaxed. "There were only some twigs in it. And—"

"Twigs!" Mr Grimshaw stared. "Twigs?"

Bernie balanced his mug on his knee, and the way he sat, head tilted, his eyes on Daniel, made us all look at him.

"Twigs?" he said.

Bernie's hair – after his hard work upstairs – stood on end. In a comical way it made him look terrified.

Mr Grimshaw turned on Bernie. "If you got summat worth saying, Bernie Kemp," he said, "spit it out. Don't wait for an invitation."

Bernie stared at the farmer. He drank. He rubbed a soot-black finger round the rim of his mug. He gazed away, nodding.

He said, "Right."

And drank again.

"Right?" cried Mr Grimshaw. "Is that it? Right? He does that! Goes over all wise-looking, and comes out with nothing but hot air!"

"I've seen twigs before," said Bernie.

"Ah," nodded Mr Grimshaw.

Daniel caught my glance, and he almost smiled. But we both knew what Bernie meant.

"Remember we put up the new barn, Able? Top of Ebenezer's Rise, what? nine years ago?"

Mr Grimshaw nodded.

"What's Ebenezer's Rise?" I asked.

"A field," said Mr Grimshaw. "Far side of Bosky Wood."

"Across the road?" asked Daniel. "Through the iron gate?"

"Beyond that," said the farmer. "Through the iron gate, right enough. Then follow the edge of the wood for quarter of a mile. There's a stream with a bridge my grandfather built. Durned thing keeps falling down. Over the bridge and round the corner of the wood, if you know what I mean, and you're onto Ebenezer's Rise. I'm sorry, Bernie. He just waits when someone interrupts. Tell us about the barn."

"We didn't want none o' that corrugated iron, did we, Able? We wanted a real old-fashioned barn built o' God's good timber.

70

That's what we wanted. Now there was timber felled nigh on twenty year ago out o' Bosky Wood. Though even in them days you had to cut your way in through the undergrowth. Was it your grandfather again, Able? I believe it was. That's right, he was touching ninety, but still making things. Took down who knows how many oak out of the wood. Got it all sawed up, then died, and nobody else had time nor patience for building whatever-it-was he was thinking of building."

Bernie placed his mug on the table and scowled.

"More tea?" I asked.

"He's thinking," said Mr Grimshaw. "I know. It was a garage—"

"That's it," said Bernie. "Keen on cars, was the old man. That garage out there – " Bernie's thumb swung towards the garage where I'd found the hose. " – wasn't enough. He wanted a new garage with space for ten or more cars. Not that he had ten cars, nor nothing like it – and a pit for working under them. But he cut a heap o' timber out o' Bosky Wood. Next to Ebenezer's Rise.

"An' he left it to weather. New-cut timber's no use. The sap has to be dried out it. Else it warps and splits. So you season it. Quick way's in a kiln, but them were mighty timbers. Too big for any kiln hereabouts. So it was left to the weather."

"Were you there?" asked Daniel.

"Both of us." Bernie nodded at Mr Grimshaw. "But only so's to humour the old man. We weren't interested in his garage. And we was none too sure about cutting trees out of Bosky Wood.

"Anyway. After Able's grandfather died – was your dad still alive then? No? No, I reckon not. The timber got left in Ebenezer's Rise. We looked after it, of course. Even in them days oak was a terrible price to buy. But it was safe enough. Nobody but us ever went near the place, and it ain't overlooked by any road or house. Here, what was I going to tell you?"

"About the barn!" I couldn't help laughing, and Bernie smiled so sweetly that I touched his sooty hand.

"The barn!" he said shyly. "And the noise it made."

"The noise?" said Daniel.

"I remember that," grunted Mr Grimshaw. "As soon as the last nail went in – Oh. There I go again. Carry on, Bernie. It's your story."

"Able's right," said Bernie. "Soon as the last nail went in, near enough. We heard nothing while the barn was being built. 'Tweren't just us working on it, you understand. Hired in some chaps, we did, who knew something about oak. But after they left, this noise started. You could hear it all round Ebenezer's Rise. A thin noise, it was, and maybe hid by the sound of hammering and sawing while we wor building the place – though we weren't hammering and sawing all the time..." Bernie smiled again.

"Tell us about the noise!" I said. "Please."

"Aye. The noise was thin, as I say. Not like something was nearby making a noise. More like lots of things, far off, whispering and tapping. Only it weren't far off. Fair gave Able the willies, eh, Able? But it didn't bother me. S'far as I wor concerned it wor just a noise."

I slipped a glance at Daniel.

His mouth was a hard little circle of flesh. If that was a sign of fear, I didn't wonder, remembering that he'd run from whispering things the night before last.

"We wor in an' out the barn all the time, as you can imagine," said Bernie, "while the building was going on. Then – as I say – when the chaps we'd hired was gone, and the rubbish burning on a bank o' the stream, and me and Able gathering up the tools into the trailer... Able walked away. His hearing's alus been a shade quicker than mine. Off he went. Ain't that right, Able? Not fast, but steady. Over his granda's bridge and round the corner of Bosky Wood he marched. I never asked him how he was feeling. I could tell. I never asked, did I, Able?

"I let him go.

"I remember stretching into the trailer with

a mallet in my hand, with the edge of the trailer pressing into my arm. The noise reached me then. Maybe it did scare me a bit, 'cos I held on to the mallet, rather than putting it away. Then I wandered towards the barn. Really, I thought a breeze was stirring through Bosky Wood, but I couldn't feel no breeze, and the sound was loudest around the barn door, and me being only a skip and jump *from* the door, why! in I went.

"I remember yet the smell of the timber. We'd been sawing nigh on a month, and the scent just filled the place! So I stood for a mo' enjoying it, then I noticed that the hay loft wor mighty dark. It was bright day outside and my eyes they hadn't adjusted, but the hay loft was a mite too dark, and I popped up the stairs – I'd put the last step in, myself, that morning – and found *things* all around me."

Bernie smiled. Mr Grimshaw tumbled more tea into Bernie's mug, then offered the teapot around.

"Don't ask what sort o' things," sighed Bernie. "You'd think Bosky Wood had sprouted fresh inside our barn. Rustling and whispering, twigs prodding me all around, yet when I reached for them—"

"You tried to *touch* them!" gasped Daniel.

Bernie tipped his ear towards Daniel, and Daniel shook his head.

"Go on!" I said.

"I couldn't get to grips with 'em. They crumbled into dust. I couldn't understand it – not one bit! An' all that rustling stirred my nerves. I ain't never been nervous. Creepy-crawlies don't bother me none. Never been afraid of the dark. Why, one of the best nights o' my life I spent the fag-end of a-sleeping off two quarts o' cider on top of Plough John's grave – and him so fresh in it I swear the earth was still warm!"

Mr Grimshaw glared at Bernie.

"Not a lot more to tell," said Bernie. "'Cept – as I say – I was a mite nervous, which surprised me.

"You'd 'ave been shaking a bit too, I reckon, with the very air rustling with things you couldn't get hold of.

"Well, I had the mallet in my hand. I threw it. I'm not sure why. I suppose we alus want to destroy wot we don't understand.

"Then I got out. I walked to the corner of the wood. Able was waiting, halfway to the iron gate, looking back at me. I gave him a wave, and he gave me a wave. Then he walked on. I finished loading the trailer; made sure the burning rubbish was safe to leave for an hour while I ate my dinner, then I popped back into the barn.

"I couldn't hear nothing. And the hay loft was just as gloomy as it ought t've been. I went up into it anyway, for I wanted the mallet.

"The mallet was lying where I'd thrown it, and scattered around were them twigs, some longer than I could stretch. Real brittle they were. One broke into pieces when I picked it up. What kind of tree they were off, I couldn't tell, but they'd been off their mother trunk for a long time. Not a sniff of sap in them, and – as I say – dry as dust.

"So I shoved the mallet into the trailer, and kept the twigs on my lap while I drove the tractor back here to the house.

"But what with getting shaken and shivered by the movement of the tractor, there weren't nothing left but a scrap in the fold of my trousers. I suppose I just brushed that away. 'Twas a long time ago...

"But what we couldn't figure out," said Bernie, standing up, "was how them twigs got into the hay loft. Brand new barn, you see. Was *they* doing the whispering? I don't know. Maybe the mallet did catch 'em. Good tea, Able. I hope you ain't turned the stop-cock on for upstairs, or water'll be meeting me in the hall." He grinned and went out.

Mr Grimshaw shuffled in his chair.

My head bustled with curiosity, but I couldn't think of a single question.

"We'd better go," said Daniel.

Mr Grimshaw saw us into the yard.

While he was pointing out where the artist's equipment had been stored, a builder's truck pulled up, and he went off to talk to the driver.

Then a Mercedes bounced along the lane, and Mr Railford stepped out.

CHAPTER SIX

"Hello, you two." Mr Railford smiled. He shook hands. "You must be Daniel."

He was wearing what Mum calls a classic sports jacket. On some men it's old-fashioned, but not on six feet four inches of mature muscle. "What a mess," he said, and I stared at the ground, thinking he was commenting on my sizzled eyebrows and fried skin.

"I'm Eric Railford."

I heard the smile in his voice and looked up. He was introducing himself to Daniel while I stood like an embarrassed twelve-year-old. He nodded at the blackened house, and I realized he hadn't been talking about me.

He grinned, and strolled to the farmhouse and stood gazing at the damage. Then he went and spoke to Mr Grimshaw.

I said to Daniel, "He's rented our flat. He

says he's an investigator. But I don't know what he investigates. Here he comes."

He smiled down on us. His eyes moved calmly but quickly around the farmyard. I doubt if he missed anything with that glance, from our bikes, now leaning together on the garage door, to the window that Daniel had smashed to get into the burning house. He didn't stare at my legs, and I wasn't sure whether to be pleased or not.

"Tell me about the fire," he said.

"That's not what you're investigating," said Daniel bluntly, and I nudged him.

"It might be." Mr Railford looked at Daniel, then at me.

Daniel said, "You were on your way here yesterday, before the fire started."

"I know, I know. You're quite right, Daniel. Mrs Grimshaw's letter reached me a few days ago. The fire isn't why I'm here. But it may have something to do with it. Look. I need to know about this fire, about prowlers, about anything odd...?"

I knew my mouth had relaxed into a gape. I looked at Daniel. He glanced at me, then seemed to decide to be awkward.

He said, "How do you mean – odd?"

"Oh," said Mr Railford, slightly amused. "Anything out of the ordinary."

"Did my mother say something?" I asked.

He shook his head. He didn't say, "What

about?" and that made me want to tell him about the tree in the bank car park – and everything else.

Clattering came from the builder's truck as men unloaded tools and equipment.

"Look," said Mr Railford. "There's obviously something bothering you. We're just in the way, here." He flinched as Mr Grimshaw bellowed for Bernie to get down and help. "Will you come back to town with me? It's nearly four o'clock now. We could have a snack somewhere, and if you feel like talking...?"

"We've got our bikes," said Daniel.

I sighed at Daniel. "He's not usually so short with people," I explained. "But things *have* happened—"

"Stella!"

"Well, they have! And if Mr Railford can help..."

"I'll tell you what," said Mr Railford. "I'll have a wander round here and you head back to town. Where's a good place to eat?"

I smiled, but kept my mouth shut. I would let Daniel make up for his boorishness.

"There's the café in the square," he mumbled.

I said, "It'll be shut by the time we get there. Mum goes to the Mitre Hotel when she's made a sale."

"I spent last night in the Mitre," said Mr

Railford. "They would give us a good bar meal – though they don't start till six. If that's all right with Daniel?"

Daniel raised his eyebrows.

"See you there, then," said Mr Railford. "Six o'clock."

His grin included us both, and he wandered off, avoiding puddles left by the fire-fighters.

"Daniel," I said threateningly. Daniel marched away.

"Daniel!" I stood, looking as beautiful as I could, but since his back was to me, it didn't help; though when I glanced round at a silence from the builder's truck, several male faces were pointed towards me. I strode after Daniel. "What is wrong with you!"

He turned and managed a smile. "Sorry, Stella." I knew he had something else to say. "It was just the way you looked at him."

I sagged. "Daniel! He's as old as Mum! And for all I know he's married. Bound to be, in fact."

"Someone like that?"

"Someone like that," I confirmed. And he smiled a real smile. Then we fetched the painting gear from the barn beside the garage. It included some canvases, but they were wrapped in plastic, so we didn't look at them.

"We'll let Mr Railford take this stuff," said Daniel. He smiled as he said it, so I helped him place the easel, paints and paintings on the ground at the door of the Mercedes.

"Come on," said Daniel. "I want to ride. Get a breeze around my face. The sun's murder."

So we cycled, eyeing the placid view of Bosky Wood and the pasture that sometimes was full of whispering branches.

We left the bikes in our garage behind the shop, and snatched a wash before wandering into the market square. We sat in the Mitre lounge, and said we were waiting for someone.

So we waited.

Then he came, Mr Railford, with a dash of soot across his brow. He laughed when I pointed it out, then ordered food, and went to clean up. That incident relaxed us, and Daniel's jealousy disappeared. He addressed Mr Railford as "Eric", and that was all right.

We demolished soup, and Eric was about to tell us what he investigated for a living, when Mum walked in, with Mrs Roper trotting like a poodle.

When my mum walks in, nobody talks.

She wasn't a top model for nothing. The men in the lounge stood up as if the Queen had entered – Eric and Daniel among them. Envious nods and rueful smiles littered the place when Mum advanced on us, kissed me, kissed Daniel (much to his shame) and beamed on Eric.

"This is Madge," said Mum, introducing

Mrs Roper to Eric.

I was amazed at Eric's enthusiasm for Mrs Roper. Madge Roper is a kind, ignorant, nosy old gossip. But she has an eye for quality, and her boutique is top-of-the-range. So a lot of Mum's wardrobe comes from there. But I couldn't see why Eric welcomed her so warmly. "I'm glad you could both come," he said, so I guessed he had stopped at our shop, and asked Mum to bring Madge with her – though how he knew her, I couldn't think.

Madge and Mum accepted Eric's invitation to eat, and while Mum waited for her sparrow's portion of main course, Madge got stuck into a plate of soup.

We were all into the main course, when I realized that Eric and Madge were doing the talking.

"When was this?" asked Eric gently.

"Three or four nights ago! All round the house it was! Not all round, of course, because there's only the front and back, the houses being stuck to each other, but somebody was at my back windows, and somebody else was at the shop door feeling my keyhole – "

Daniel stifled a giggle.

Eric smiled kindly on Mrs Roper.

" – so I phoned the police! I've a lot of valuable stock downstairs in my shop!" Madge half-glanced at what Mum was wearing. "I don't hesitate about that! And I must say, a

83

police car was in the street in two shakes. But they didn't find anything. And I could see they weren't pleased. Two of them, there were. A policeman and a policewoman—"

"They weren't pleased?"

"I don't mean at being called out! They just weren't pleased about something. And I saw it. So I said, I hope you're not blaming me because you haven't found anybody! And they said, no, it wasn't that, but they'd been run ragged for weeks with folks calling them out, and there was never hardly a sign of prowlers. They caught one or two, I believe, but these officers seemed puzzled about the noises back and front of my house and not a footprint in the garden and not a scratch around a lock.

"Then the woman officer, she looked at the man officer, and he nodded, and she said, 'Mrs Roper' – very polite they were even though they were annoyed – 'was there anything else?' And I gave her a look. I said, 'What d'you mean? Isn't what I told you enough?' And she shook her head, and for a second I thought she meant that what had happened wasn't enough, and I was going to contradict her, for it was more than enough for me – but she touched my shoulder in a right nice way, and she said, 'Wasn't there something else? Something strange, that you're not telling us because you think we won't believe you?'"

Madge Roper rested her knife and fork.

Her hands trembled.

"I don't know how she knew," she said.

"Go on," said Eric.

"I never mentioned it. I thought I was just being a silly woman. I never told them on the phone. But when that lady officer – just a girl she was – asked me about there being something strange... I told her. I told them both." Madge stared at her food. "You see, besides the scratching at the front door and round the back, there was something tapping all over my windows; not just downstairs – that would've been bad enough – like a whole gang was round my house; but the scratching was at my upstairs windows too – fifteen feet above the pavement. Scratching and tapping, tapping and scratching. There's nothing I know of could do that! The policewoman was right – I'd thought they'd never believe me."

Madge drew in a breath, then gazed at her plate. Then she ate. I could see she was trying not to cry.

Eric turned and beckoned a waitress. He ordered drinks. Madge Roper devoured a whisky.

"Try not to get upset," said Eric. "Could you tell me a bit more?"

Madge shook her head. "There's no more to tell."

"Didn't you look out of the window?"

"That I did! When the noises stopped. I

didn't dare before! But there wasn't anybody. Not a soul! That was tasty." She stared at her whisky glass. Eric ordered her another.

Mum sipped a soda water. Daniel and I made do with fruit juice. Eric swirled a half-pint of beer around in its glass.

"Your house is in the same street as Elaine's shop?"

I narrowed my eyes at Mum; first name terms, already? Mum gave me her it-means-nothing-to-me look.

Madge frowned at her whisky. She said, "Yes."

"So your boutique faces onto the same bit of pavement as the antique shop? And at the back is your garden?"

"Yes."

"Which windows did you look out?" Eric's voice was light – hypnotic almost.

"My bedroom window."

"At the back? Tell me what you saw."

"Nothing. The garden. It was dark, of course, but plenty of starlight. And I switched on the outside light."

"Ah. What did you see then?"

"Nobody."

"I don't mean people, Mrs Roper. Just tell me what you saw."

"The garden, of course. My little lawn. The outside light's high up on the house wall. So's no one can reach it to break the bulb. But it's bright. Trees. The stone path from the back door. It goes among the trees."

"You could see the path?"

"Oh, yes. But it fades away. There's an open space – a bit of garden – where the pears grow against the wall. Over the wall – over several walls, I mean – is Mr Hilary the grocer. You'll meet him. He pops into Elaine's for coffee most days."

Eric was nodding. "I believe I saw Mr Hilary just after lunchtime today, when I arrived at Elaine's shop."

Mum nodded too, but didn't interrupt. I think she sensed that Eric Railford was speaking in this quiet way, quite deliberately.

Madge Roper had forgotten her food. Her fingers lay relaxed around her whisky glass.

"I don't want to suggest anything," murmured Eric. "But think of the trees. Were they— ?"

"The trees," sighed Madge. "I can see them now. I can see the path, made of stone slabs. And … tree roots on the path. I thought, a body could fall over that. I wondered why I hadn't. Only the day before, I was weeding between the slabs. It was funny, you know, not noticing those roots. But we don't notice things that creep up on us in life, do we? Until they get a hold. Like old age."

"Quite right." Eric drank his beer.

Madge seemed to wake out of a dream.

"Would you mind terribly," said Eric to Madge, "if I had a look at your garden?"

"You like gardens?"

"I'm interested in all sorts of things," smiled Eric. His smile moved to my mother.

"Do you mean this evening?" said Madge.

"Mm. After we've finished eating. If that's all right."

"I think I've a bottle of whisky somewhere." Madge laughed, and Eric beamed.

But we were not invited.

CHAPTER SEVEN

Daniel and I dawdled into the square and sat on the wall that borders the cathedral lawn. Heat radiated from the cathedral's stones. The cedars stood still as if afraid to breathe the evening's dusty air.

I looked at the bin that Daniel had refused to walk to the day before yesterday. I could have lobbed an apple core into it – if I'd had an apple core. It's hard to believe in spooky things when cars are wandering through the market square, and passers-by are passing by. I could see no reason for hordes of twigs haunting our town. And if Susie Kelso was to be believed, they weren't limited to the town – or to just now. She had seen "crabs" at Cromer, years ago.

"We didn't tell Eric," said Daniel, "about Bosky Wood."

"We didn't get the chance," I said. "He went all cosy with Madge Roper. D'you think he knew that she'd seen something?"

Daniel leaned his shoulder against mine. "What do you mean?"

"He seemed to suspect," I said, "that Madge hadn't told the police everything."

"You mean about the tree roots on her garden path? Same as I saw on the road to Bosky. Yes..." Daniel took my hand casually. "Susie was right," he said, "those things don't belong in this world. I think that's why I was so terrified..." He hunched his shoulders. "Ugh," he said.

From the far side of the square, a man waved at me. Not a "Hello, Stella!" wave, but an "I'm here," wave. He was short, and I think, lean, but for some reason, I couldn't see him properly. Perhaps because the sun was lower over the rooftops, and dazzling. Maybe he was wearing a shirt with short sleeves.

I knew better than to encourage strangers.

"Come on!" I said to Daniel.

"Where are we going?"

I dragged him by the fingers. "Home. We'll pick up Susie's bike and take it to her."

We wandered round the corner of the cathedral wall out of the square.

We paused at Madge Roper's boutique, and looked in at her display of clothes. Eric was probably upstairs sharing her whisky. Mum would be at home polishing our antiques. She avoids Madge's drinking bouts.

We went to our garage. I left my hat there, because cycling was easier without it. We pedalled back through the square and out the other side. I'd forgotten about the man who had waved. In five minutes we had delivered Susie's bike, and were on the pavement outside her door, me wheel-less, and Daniel saying, "I'll see you home."

"Your mum will be wondering where you are."

Daniel made a face.

"She won't know you've eaten," I insisted.

"The chip fat will be smoking," grinned Daniel.

"You whizz off," I said. "Tell your mum you're coming to my place for the evening. We must show the tube of twigs to Eric. I'll hang around the square. I want to see the price of that jacket in Jenner's window."

"OK. Ten minutes, Stella."

I wandered back to the square. The traffic was less. The cathedral clock clanged quarter past seven. The only people around were two soldiers in uniform staring up at the cathedral tower. Soldiers were an oddity in our town, but I didn't bother to think about them.

Jenner's window always tempted me. It's across the square from the cathedral. I bent my head to read the price on the jacket.

If the psychology of unreadable price tickets is to lure the customer in – it doesn't work. We're far from poor, but if a shop won't tell you the price, then it must be too much. I turned away.

The little lean man was standing under a cedar tree in the cathedral grounds.

He saw me.

At least I think he saw me, because I still couldn't see him properly, so I peered, wondering why the sunlight and shadows were so confusing.

I looked along the road; Daniel would be five minutes at least – if his mother didn't stuff a glass of milk and a sandwich into him; then he would be ten minutes.

I faced Jenner's window again. I stared at the reflections in the glass thinking I would see the man. The cathedral's bulk shone clearly, but the darkness of the cedars dissolved into gowns and perching shoes.

I walked along the pavement. The man didn't seem threatening, but I hoped my shorts weren't as tight as Susie Kelso's.

I glanced back, pretending to look at the cathedral clock. The man was on the path beside the bin. Perhaps the heat coming off the cathedral's stones affected the air, because I still couldn't focus on him. Then he blurred and vanished.

I blinked.

For a second, I didn't know what to think.

Then I wondered if my eyes had been damaged by the fire at Grimshaw's.

But, of course, the man hadn't vanished; he was on the pavement in front of the cathedral.

I frowned. How could he have walked the few steps to the pavement, in full view, without my seeing him?

My heart thudded suddenly at the thought of my eyes being wonky, and I stared up at the cathedral clock.

Then I sighed with relief. Eighteen and a quarter minutes past seven. Nothing wrong with my sight – thank goodness!

I looked across the square.

The little man was on the road.

A car approached him, but he seemed not to hear it, and – my heart bumping again – I drew in a breath to yell.

But the car shot past as if he didn't exist.

He should have been flattened, but he was now halfway across the square, and waving at me.

I didn't understand this.

I turned, and hurried along the pavement. Something very weird was happening.

I knew that the little man wasn't a ghost, because there's no such thing. He was just an ordinary person dressed for the summer weather, but rather blurry because of the light (or something), and capable of moving

93

so fast that I kept losing sight of him. Which was brilliant.

Then I realized that I was walking away from Daniel.

On the opposite pavement the soldiers approached the Mitre. Their presence reassured me, so I turned and marched back towards the man, determined to face him.

But he was gone.

The pavement was empty. The square was empty – except for a car or two.

He wasn't lurking in a shop doorway.

I swear that the pavement was empty except for dust and bus tickets.

Then he was walking towards me. Along the pavement. That's right: he wasn't there – then he was.

Then – you know how bicycle spokes blur and vanish as the wheels spin faster? That's what he did. I don't mean he spun – but he blurred and vanished. He came towards me at the same time.

I couldn't think what was happening. I shrieked and turned away.

Then my face went numb with shock. As I said, I turned, and twenty paces ahead of me was the little man looking back over his shoulder; somehow, he had passed me.

Well. I ran.

I fled across the square.

The soldiers pushed into the Mitre; they

obviously hadn't heard me cry out.

As I ran, I looked for Daniel, but there was no sign of him.

I raced into our street. Then I pictured the little man glancing over his shoulder at me, and thought that maybe he was as bewildered as I was.

So I walked, frowning.

Was there really something wrong with my eyes? I looked back. Our bendy little street appeared as sharp as usual.

But still no Daniel.

I let myself in to the lobby at the foot of the stairs.

I pushed through the green baize door and looked out from the shop window.

One or two people were about, but not the man – though perhaps a shadow moved in the middle of the road.

Mum and Eric were in the sitting-room above the shop.

"You weren't long at Madge's," I said to Eric, trying to smile. "Did you find out anything?"

Eric shrugged. I guessed he'd been enjoying talking to my mother, and I had interrupted.

The front door buzzer sounded. We have a speaker system. I answered it.

"It's me," said Daniel. "Sorry."

"I'll come down."

I let him in. "Sorry," he said. "My mother…"

He gathered me close, forgetting his mother,

and used his mouth to warm mine. He hauled my body against his. I pushed his face aside. "Daniel! That man followed me!"

"What man?"

"The man in the square!"

Daniel hadn't noticed him.

I explained, and he shook his head. "It's too crazy for me, Stella."

I said, "I'm heading for the shower. Knock before you go into the sitting-room."

The bathroom is at the top of the flight of stairs, on the same landing as the house kitchen; Daniel came with me as far as the kitchen; through the kitchen and round a couple of corners would take him to the sitting-room.

After showering, I peeped from the bathroom onto the landing. Wearing a towel, and carrying my clothes, I trotted up the five steps to the top landing. The laundry basket (Indian, late twentieth century, bought by me in the local tourist shop) decorates a corner beside my kitchen door. I dropped the clothes onto the basket lid, and stepped into my bedroom.

Something was wrong.

My naked arms goose-bumped instantly.

I screwed the towel tight over my chest. My toes dug themselves into the carpet.

Evening sunlight glowed on the mellow colours of the chest-of-drawers.

A shadow beside the oak press (which I used as a wardrobe) stood transparent enough for me to see dust drifting.

Mrs Grimshaw's wooden tube with its spilled twigs lay within my reach on the dressing table.

In other words – the room was normal. Except that the heat of my shower was being sucked off my skin.

I thought of the tapping things, and stared hard to see if they lurked, perhaps, behind the Charles II chair with the high back; but only the wallpaper clung to the walls. Only carpet lay in the corners, and only the movement of sunlight over my bed caused any visible change.

I thought of running; then I remembered the towel around me, and decided I would not leave my bedroom without clean clothes.

The clothes were in the chest-of-drawers. To get to the chest I would have to walk between the dressing table and the end of my bed. Four paces.

Maybe five.

What a long walk! I thought. Five whole paces across the bedroom I'd lived in all my life. And that walk, I realized, would bring me closer to the shadow with the dust drifting – though I could see nothing wrong with the shadow.

As I thought these bright thoughts, I

stepped – counting, one step, two, three. In my nervousness, I stepped tinily and needed six steps to reach the chest-of-drawers. And the goose bumps heaved themselves up on my skin. I clung to the towel with one hand, and half-turned from the shadow to open the drawer.

My fingers didn't reach the drawer.

As I turned towards it, on the edge of my vision, I saw something in the shadow.

I jerked upright.

My throat closed in fear.

Peering around the press, half-dissolved in the shadow, was a human eye.

CHAPTER EIGHT

I didn't remember going down the top flight. I didn't hear myself screaming until I reached Mum's kitchen, and Eric, Daniel and my mother burst in to meet me. I knew then I was screaming. I ignored their questions. My eyes felt huge, and my face must have been white for I could feel the blood drawn down to my heart. I pointed.

Eric ran. Daniel gaped. He looked at my shoulders, then at my legs. He dashed after Eric. Mum grabbed me, lifted me clear of the floor and swept me into her bedroom. Then her dressing-gown was round me and I was sitting in her embrace on the bed.

We sat, Mum cooing, me shaking.

"Stella?" Eric's voice.

"In here!" called Mum, and Eric came in cautiously, Daniel bobbing behind his shoulder.

Eric raised his eyebrows at me.

I stared at him. I looked at Daniel.

Daniel said, "Stella?"

I quavered, "Well?"

"We didn't see anything," said Eric. "Is she all right?"

"I think so," said Mum, leaning away from me to look at my face. "Her colour's coming back. Stella?"

A gasp escaped my lungs. "Mum! You know that medicine you fed Daniel and me in the middle of the night…?"

"She's better," said my mother. "I'll fetch your clothes." And she went, and I loved her more than ever for not asking what was wrong. She directed Eric to the sitting-room, and left Daniel gaping at me.

"What happened, Stella!" cried Daniel. He sat where Mum had warmed the bed and put his arms round me. If he needed an excuse, my shaky state was a good one. I sank against him. He hugged me, asking what was wrong. I was conscious of being naked, except for the towel, under Mum's dressing-gown. My toes curled into the carpet again, but this time, for different feelings.

"Clothes!" said Mum. "Daniel!" Daniel moved out of the room.

"Should I stay?" asked Mum.

I shook my head.

"Eric is pouring your medicine." She

watched me.

"I'll be through in a minute. Thanks." And she left, and I got dressed.

I had seen an eye.

Not a face. Just an eye, drifting in the shadow of the press. Looking at me. A blue eye? I think it was blue. Was I crazy? I zipped my skirt, and headed for the sitting-room.

The whisky sank with healing warmth.

I told Mum, Daniel and Eric how I had felt chilled, and what I had seen.

"Better show me where," said Eric rising. So we trailed through the kitchen and up the five steps to my bedroom. I went in carefully. But it was just my old bedroom, cosy as ever. I told my story again, with actions.

Eric stood where I had seen the eye, and stared at me. "Here, Stella?" he asked.

"Lower."

He crouched.

"Lower yet. There." His eyes were level with that eye.

Eric felt the top of his head, then touched the press to mark his height. "Five feet six, at a guess. I want to measure this more accurately. Excuse me, Stella."

I let him pass between me and the bed-end. "Measure what?" I asked.

He stopped, looking at the twigs on the dressing-table. He said vacantly, "The height of the person in the shadow. What are these?"

"You believe me?"

"Oh, yes. What are these?"

"Just twigs. They were in that wooden tube. Mrs Grimshaw gave it to Daniel. You really believe that someone—?"

"Did she now!" Eric crouched and peered at the twigs without touching them.

He took a flat plastic box from his jacket pocket. It swivelled open into a magnifying glass. He examined the twigs through the glass.

"Have you handled these?" he asked.

"No," said Daniel. He didn't say that just looking at them gave us the creeps.

"Then they're not contaminated with your sweat. Possibly make-up off the dressing-table, though, and dust."

I didn't know what Eric was talking about.

"Back in a minute!" He swept out, thudded up to his apartment, and was back carrying a glass bottle that looked as if it belonged in a laboratory. He used his pen to ease the twigs into the bottle; he sealed them inside with a rubber stopper. Then he produced a measuring tape, and confirmed five feet six on the side of my press. Or, a hundred and sixty-eight centimetres.

We returned to the sitting-room, Eric carrying the bottle.

"You know what these are?" Eric held the bottle delicately.

I shook my head, and my face heated up as I

remembered Daniel kissing me immediately after the twigs had spilled from the tube. We had avoided discussing the twigs.

Eric smiled, and my heart stood on its head. He really was gorgeous. I looked at Mum. She was staring at the carpet, pretending she wasn't blushing. (Mum – being a red-head – tends to blush.)

Eric laid the bottle on its side so that the twigs were lying down.

Sunlight probed the ancient furniture. A single oak beam divided the ceiling.

Daniel and I sat on the sofa, me with my medicine, Daniel refusing anything to drink.

Eric poured Mum a small port and himself a whisky. He relaxed all six foot four inches of himself into an armchair, and looked as if he belonged. My mother's glance rested on him. Perhaps she, too, thought that he belonged.

"Cheers!" whispered Eric. "Here's to spooks. Here's to…" He smiled gently at Mum. "Here's to the future." A glow of embarrassment burned on his cheek bones.

We waited.

Eric stared at his shoes.

"If you've something to tell us," said my mother, "we're listening."

"I always find this difficult."

"Do start."

"It's no big deal, but I always feel rather … sneaky. I don't mean to be, but my job is pretty confidential, and I'm in touch with so many people who give me information. For example, the police, who told me about Madge Roper's prowlers, and – " He shrugged with embarrassment. " – I probably know more about this house than you do."

Mum's eyebrows went up.

"Hadn't you better start at the beginning?" she said in her cool voice.

"Yes," admitted Eric, "but – oh, well." He looked into our waiting faces. "I am Brigadier Eric Monteray Railford."

"Brigadier!" I said, remembering the soldiers in the square.

"I'm an army officer, Stella; but mainly I'm a mathematician. The rank is to give me authority when I need it, and back-up. My job is investigating what no one else investigates, and I am here because of a letter sent by Mrs Grimshaw to the Queen."

He slid a finger along the bottle containing the twigs. He waited for comments, but no one spoke.

"You'd be surprised how many people write to the Queen." He laughed.

We still didn't say anything, so he went on.

"Mrs Grimshaw's letter was passed to me. I decided that she was not talking through a hole in her hat when she reported that Bosky Wood was ... disturbed, and that the disturbances were increasing. So I wrote to

104

her, and got her to invite me down here. The phenomena, you see – though Mrs Grimshaw doesn't know this – coincides with events in Norfolk in the early seventeenth century."

Daniel frowned, but managed not to speak.

"Under Horse Guards Parade," said Eric, "are archives containing top secret documents written from 1590 onwards, by a mathematician named Ebenezer Bagge.

"These documents are secret because they contain – besides diaries covering several decades – mathematical treatises which could be extremely dangerous. They already have caused distress to the man who wrote them, and to people who lived after him. Ebenezer lived in Norfolk – "

I decided that Eric was used to lecturing; he sounded like our headmaster.

" – and he was the most extraordinary kind of mathematician, having – what we would call today – a computer mind. The answers to complex equations appeared in his head and he simply wrote them down.

"Ebenezer conceived the idea of a parallel universe. Which is – " he murmured, as Daniel shifted on the sofa " – another universe co-existent with ours. H.G. Wells had the same idea early this century: our earth exists here, and another earth exists in the same space. That's the theory. And if another earth, why not another universe? A very strange concept."

I gathered Daniel's fingers in mine, and we sat back into the sofa. I think that was the moment when something changed for Daniel and me.

We had been kids together in primary school, and had shared our homes all our lives, but now, with the weird events of the last couple of days drawing us together, and Eric talking so oddly…

And – I suppose – we were growing up.

Daniel saw my look, and his mouth closed around a smile. His fingers sent a message through my nerves.

"Ebenezer," continued Eric, "worked at his calculations for twenty-seven years."

"Twenty-seven years!" I whispered.

"Then in 1617 Ebenezer commenced his Great Experiment. You see, the next logical step to proving the existence of another dimension – is to go into that dimension."

I clung to Daniel's hand until our wrists crossed.

"The Great Experiment," said Eric, "was the culmination of many lesser experiments. These experiments used light, lenses and mirrors. His lenses were an improvement even on those of Kepler, and his mathematics, of course, pre-dated everyone. We're only coming to grips with his mathematics now. The early experiments involved sending objects and animals into the…" Eric smiled. "…wherever."

"He succeeded?" whispered Daniel.

"Oh, yes. Which didn't do his reputation any good. Someone who could make animals disappear was a witch. Especially when these animals did not disappear entirely, but could be observed when the light was right, still occupying their favourite places. For example, Ebenezer purchased a sow from a neighbouring farmer, sent it into the outer darkness, and saw for himself – after complaints from the farmer – that the pig had returned to its sty – except that no one could lay hands on it, because it had no substance. It is said today, that a sow snuffles around the foot of a streetlamp in Upper Saxtead. Which is where Ebenezer lived."

"But surely – " from Daniel.

Eric's eye landed on Daniel. "I have been to Upper Saxtead," he stated. "I have heard a sound which is very like a pig snuffling. Though, I admit, that not everyone can hear it. Some phenomena are only seen (or heard) by people who are sensitive."

I thought of Susie Kelso.

"But there are more instances," said Eric. "*Hundreds* of them. I have experienced many strange things all around that area. The fact that the pig appeared in its sty suggests that the parallel world is the same as this. In other words, as far as the pig was concerned, it was back in its usual sty, though, in fact it was in the corresponding sty in—"

"The Place Between," I said.

"An identical earth," sighed Daniel.

"Yes. Anyway, Daniel, Stella – as I said – in 1617 Ebenezer was in danger of being hanged as a witch. So he retreated from Norfolk to … um … here."

Eric produced a tight smile for my mother.

"You mean to this town?" she asked.

"Ye-es," said Eric.

"He means to this house!" I cried. "Don't you?"

"Let me tell you what happened. You're quite right, Stella, Ebenezer moved into this house. I think I mentioned, Elaine, that it was particularly convenient that Mrs Grimshaw directed me here." Eric paused, and I knew he was thinking that it was convenient being near my mother, as well as living in the house that had once belonged to Ebenezer Bagge.

"But," continued Eric, "Ebenezer didn't want to make the same mistake as last time, that is, get himself accused of witchcraft. So he bought another house besides this one. Exactly where, I'm not sure, because – of course – most houses of that time are gone. But he bought the other house out of town so that he could experiment in peace, but this – " Eric's arm enclosed all four floors of our house and antique shop. " – was his home. His family lived here, and the servants.

"He couldn't begin the Great Experiment immediately. Long preparations were necessary, and because he had moved to an unfamiliar landscape, the preparations begun in Norfolk were, to some extent, no use to him. The configuration of the landscape was vital if he was to align his instruments correctly."

"It's a bit fantastic," mumbled Daniel.

"It's totally fantastic," agreed Eric, and a glow shone in his cheeks. He whispered, "His equations are beautiful, like..."

His eyes danced, and I thought he was about to quote poetry; then he looked at me as if to say, Well, never mind.

"Ebenezer," he continued, "began his new calculations. Not twenty-seven years' worth – a couple of years. Measuring every detail of the countryside. Improving his instruments. And hesitating. Yes, Stella, hesitating; because news was reaching him from Upper Saxtead of new, unexpected phenomena.

"And not only from Upper Saxtead. Within months, reports came from the whole of East Anglia. Then Cambridgeshire and Lincoln. Reports of prowlers no one ever saw – same as here; and forests whispering. Do you know that Bosky Wood is the remnant of an ancient forest? Mm. And twigs, taller than houses, gathering in open spaces. Stella? Something wrong?"

"Tell you after." I was bursting to mention

the twigs that had chased Daniel from Bosky Wood to our shop, but I wanted to hear about Ebenezer. Where had I heard that name before?

"Ebenezer – " Eric narrowed his glance at me. " – realized two things.

"First. That his experiments so far – which had opened a door between our world and the parallel world – had left the door open. Or – to put it another way – the door was now opening and closing of its own accord, because its stability had been disturbed by the experiments. But please understand: When I say a door, I don't mean an entrance that is fixed in space or time. It is something which is adjusting and changing constantly – often touching our world in many places at once. This explains the increased phenomena in Norfolk in Ebenezer's time.

"Secondly, Ebenezer realized that if the twigs had come from … The Place Between, then the door he had opened to the other world was not one-way. Which was good news, because it meant that – theoretically – if he went through, he could return. Perhaps," he said, his voice suddenly quiet as if he were thinking out loud, "he did go through. But he certainly didn't return… Anyway – "

Eric put down his whisky. He reached for the laboratory bottle containing the twigs.

What he was about to say, I didn't know;

I wanted to ask about Ebenezer perhaps going into The Place Between, but Eric's cheeks shone again, and his eyes swept around us in excitement. He reached a hand towards Mum, but she didn't move, though her gaze stayed on his face.

He lowered his hand onto the jar.

"These twigs," he said, his voice rising, "are – I believe – parts of living beings from another universe."

CHAPTER NINE

My mind clouded over.

There are some things you can't take in. A hundred thoughts gathered, all wanting my attention – but I couldn't catch any one of them to put it into words.

Perhaps Mum and Daniel felt the same, for silence dragged its feet through the sitting-room.

Then chatter broke loose.

Daniel proclaimed his now-hold-on-a-minute-while-we-think-this-through attitude; Mum requested more explanations, and I gabbled about the man who had waved to me in the square because I didn't know what to say about other universes, but wanted my share of the talking anyway.

My mother – I discovered amid the noise – had told Eric about Daniel and Susie's picnic at Bosky Wood; and Eric demanded that Daniel should tell the whole story again. Which he did, and on the retelling, we realized that the things which had followed Daniel were the same things which Eric knew about from the old Norfolk stories – the things in Mrs Grimshaw's wooden tube – though we still didn't know where she had got them... Wow.

Then I had to tell Eric – calmly – about the man in the square. He nodded over this, but didn't offer an explanation.

What Eric didn't know was Bernie Kemp's tale of noises in the barn. So we told him that too, me shutting up, to let Daniel recall Bernie's words.

At the mention of Ebenezer's Rise, Eric pushed out a smile which warmed the house. Ebenezer's Rise – surely! – was named after Ebenezer Bagge!

Eric asked the location of Ebenezer's Rise. He suggested we take a look in the morning.

At the mention of morning, Mum suggested supper to Eric, and the mood for fantasy was broken; and when Mother elbowed me with a glance, I grabbed Daniel, made us toast (eventually) in my kitchen, acknowledged our closer relationship with a kiss, and threw him out.

Then sleep pulled me down, and I knew nothing until sunlight stood in my bedroom as cheerful as kittens. I grinned as I clattered down to the bathroom for my shower; then I sang as I invaded Mum's kitchen; and in she came, beaming.

I said, "He is nice."

She said, "Mm."

I said, "So is Daniel."

The look she gave me was not mother-to-daughter, but woman-to-woman – more or less. So I assured her I would take my time over Daniel. Then I asked – just to be certain – whether Eric was married, and he wasn't; never found the right girl.

So that was OK.

Morning lay hard and bright on Bosky Wood.

I stared out from Eric's Mercedes as we swung into the lane to Grimshaw's farm. Daniel was out of the car first and running to look at the front of the house. The builder's truck stood with its tail down, and timber half-slid onto the ground.

"They've rebuilt some of the wall already!" called Daniel. "Mrs Grimshaw'll be pleased."

Thudding sounded upstairs, and a hammer flashed against new beams in the roof.

Eric led us round the back of the house. The barn reminded me of the paints and easel which I hadn't seen since I'd left them beside the Mercedes. Maybe I would honour Bosky Wood with a portrait of itself.

Eric wanted to get permission from Mr Grimshaw to look at the new barn – that is, the one that Bernie Kemp helped build nine years ago.

What happened next is awkward to explain, because it was slightly odd.

Mr Grimshaw had been in his shirt sleeves when we drank tea in his kitchen the day before, and now, as Eric thumped the back door of the farmhouse and called out above the hammering, a man in shirt sleeves walked into the barn. I only glimpsed him, because I was really looking at the damaged house.

I said, "Mr Grimshaw's gone into the barn."

"Has he?" said Eric. "I didn't see anyone."

"I saw him," said Daniel. "But I didn't see where he came from." He noticed me frowning at him. "What?"

I asked, "Why did you say that you saw him?"

Daniel smiled, not understanding.

I said, "Sorry. I'm being silly."

But maybe I wasn't being silly; Daniel had spoken as if there was some doubt about my seeing Mr Grimshaw – or else why confirm it?

We walked into the barn, and stopped.

Dust soared in the hot morning air.

Hay bales made giant steps to nowhere.

Mainly, the barn was full of emptiness. The only exit was where we were standing. So unless Mr Grimshaw had buried himself under the hay bales, he had – despite the lack of exits – got out again within ten seconds of entering.

I reached for Daniel's hand.

"Stay here," murmured Eric.

He walked into the barn's emptiness. He stepped hugely up one staircase of bales – but there was nowhere to go. He descended and went up another. He shook a bale by its shoulder, but it told him nothing. He looked into the roof space. He called to us, "Are you sure it was Mr Grimshaw?"

"He was in shirt sleeves!" I called. "Same height…"

Daniel nodded.

"Take a look!" called Eric, so we wandered, and sat on the bales. We shrugged a lot, and raised our eyebrows, then returned to the yard.

"You both saw him," said Eric. "Stella was right, Daniel. Why did you say that you saw him? If everything was normal you wouldn't have felt the need to mention it."

"Surprise, I suppose. I didn't see him arrive. He appeared in the corner of my eye and disappeared into the barn. And I suppose I wasn't sure it was him. But when Stella said…"

"Let's just find Grimshaw, shall we?" murmured Eric, and when the hammering under the roof stopped, he knocked on the back door of the house, opened it, and shouted.

"Somebody's coming."

Feet clumped down the staircase. Mr Grimshaw, with a hammer in his belt, welcomed us.

"Busy?" said Eric politely.

"Hard work, that roof. But things are taking shape. The lads are going at it, so the worst'll be over by the time Grace gets out of hospital. Doing fine, she is, thanks. But I don't know." The farmer eased his back. "When I ask her about how the fire started, she changes the subject. I told her, 'We've got to know,' I said, 'for the insurance.' But she chatters on – mainly about you, Mr Railford. Would you speak to her? She won't tell me."

"Of course," smiled Eric. "I'll pop into the hospital later today. Mr Grimshaw, have you been down in the yard here, in the last few minutes?"

"No."

"Anyone else?"

"No. No, Bernie's up under the roof. So's the two lads off the truck. Did you see someone?"

"We thought we did. But there was nobody. Could we look at the new barn? The one at Bosky Wood?"

"Help yourself! Anything you need, help yourself. Leave your car here. When you're done we'll have a cup of tea. And I'll tell you this – when the house is fixed and Grace is up to it, you'll come here for the biggest meal you ever saw in your life. That's a promise. Now, I must get on. See you later. See you later, Stella. Daniel." And he turned indoors.

We wandered back along the lane towards the main road.

The sun stung my face. I pulled my hat forward. Daniel walked close at my elbow. Eric, at times, walked backwards, taking in every detail of the landscape. He shaded his eyes to stare at Bosky Wood. Even in the brilliance of the morning, the trees made a menacing hump among the fields. But that was just my imagination.

We climbed the iron gate. Daniel pointed out where he and Susie Kelso had left their bikes, and where the tree had stood between the tractor tracks.

Eric paused on the mound, the tree stumps among the stones poised like frozen-legged creatures about to scuttle away. He crouched and touched one of the cut stones; then we walked on, Daniel and I keeping beyond the reach of the trees in the wood, Eric pushing aside the briar which straggled through the wood's boundary fence, to peer into the gloom below the foliage.

But he said nothing, and we found Grandfather Grimshaw's bridge, and crossed a stream which came out of Bosky Wood.

Then we walked around the corner of the wood, paddling on the edge of a sea of corn;

and Eric encouraged us to admire the "new" nine-year-old barn. I wish that was all we had done.

But we didn't.

We went inside.

I saw blotches in the barn's gloom.

Then my eyes cleared, and a ladder led my gaze up to the hay loft where Bernie had thrown the mallet. He had gathered the twigs there.

I wondered where the twigs had come from that Mrs Grimshaw had given Daniel in the wooden tube. Perhaps we would find out today when we visited the hospital. It was time I visited Mrs Grimshaw. I cringed at my own selfishness.

Daniel jumped up to sit on a wooden trestle. The trestle was grooved with saw cuts.

"It's creepy," I whispered, and Eric looked at me.

"It is a bit," he agreed. He prodded some sacks that dozed in a corner. "Cattle feed." He wandered to the foot of the ladder. "It is creepy," he murmured.

Sunlight streamed in through vents in the wooden walls, making a dazzling haze of shadow. I wanted to wipe the dazzle away to see into the faint distances of the barn.

Daniel amused himself by vaulting over the trestle.

Eric was on the first rung of the ladder.

Ladders have never bothered me; but I will carry into my old age the image of Eric, with his hair ruffled, one foot on the lowest rung and the sunlight piercing the gloom.

He began to climb.

His elegant jacket flapped open.

I knew something was going to happen. But I didn't call out. I counted the rungs as he went up. One ... two. Three. Four.

On the fifth he hesitated.

He looked down at me, as if puzzled. His lips moved in the shape of my name.

Six.

I don't know how to say it.

Daniel vaulted the trestle, and thudded onto the floor.

As Eric pulled himself onto the sixth rung, his head disappeared.

CHAPTER TEN

Oh, crazy! crazy! crazy! I know how it sounds! I shrieked! He went on climbing. Seven! Eight! Nine! His shoulders vanished. He was swallowed down to the waist. I screamed, but wherever his head was, he couldn't hear.

Daniel fled to the ladder. He climbed like an acrobat. He reached up.

But, ten! eleven! twelve! and Eric's polished brogues stepped upwards into nothing.

I think I went mad.

I remember throwing my hat. It swirled above the twelfth rung and vanished. I waited for it to drop into sight. But it didn't.

I tore handfuls of dust from the floor and hurled them, so that they fell in curtains through the sunlight. I think I did these things to make contact with Eric. Because my feet wouldn't move.

I screamed, and wept.

Then my feet moved.

Daniel – on the ladder – was coughing and holding his eyes because I had thrown the dust over him. I leapt onto the lower rungs. I climbed past Daniel, my head full of hate for what had happened. Seven! eight! nine! I screamed out my fury at the sunlight. Ten! eleven! twelve! And I stepped onto the hay loft.

"Stella!"

I turned and looked down. Daniel gaped up at me, his face wet with dusty tears. "He's not gone?"

"He's gone!" I screamed. My foot stamped. "He's gone! He's gone! He's gone—!"

"Stop it, Stella!"

Then Daniel was beside me. Holding me. He said, "I thought I was going to lose you too!" And we trembled.

I felt him shake from his chest to his knees. Perhaps I fainted for a second, because I was suddenly lying in a scatter of hay, and Daniel was kissing me, and I exploded kisses on his face, on his mouth, and his body pressed hard onto me, and boiling surges urged me against him; then a vision of Eric climbing into nothing drew a shriek from me. And I struggled free of Daniel, and oh! I wept, and wept, and wept.

And while I wept, I was aware of Daniel, on

his back, panting, his fingers patting my leg. Then we rolled together and kissed each other's tears.

"I need a tissue," I gulped, and searched my sleeve.

I dabbed Daniel's cheeks, then my own, and blew my nose. Daniel helped me up, and we stood hopelessly.

Eric was gone. The Place Between had eaten him, and there was nothing anyone in this world could do.

By the time we'd climbed down the ladder, I was crying again. Daniel touched my tears. "We've no more tissues," he said.

Then we walked out of the barn, and stood in the sunshine.

I said, "We can't leave him."

I let Daniel hold me. Then: "Wait," he said, and ran back into the barn.

He shouted Eric's name.

But I knew it was no use; Eric hadn't heard me calling as he disappeared up the ladder.

"Send him back!" yelled Daniel. But he said it just once.

Then he strode out, bewildered, and we walked towards Grandfather Grimshaw's bridge. The bridge was near the corner of the wood. Only when you are at the bridge can you see along the other edge of the wood to the mound and the iron gate.

I looked towards the mound. Beyond it,

someone stepped off the gate into the road and vanished behind the hedge. I only glimpsed his back; and my eyes were blurred with tears. Daniel was helping me to walk, and didn't notice.

We passed the mound.

I climbed the gate angrily.

Daniel jumped onto the tarmac.

The same person who had climbed the gate turned into the lane which led to Grimshaw's farm. I supposed it was Bernie Kemp, though why we hadn't seen him at the barn, I couldn't think because if he had climbed the gate after being in the pasture, the only place he could have been was the barn. Unless he had come into the pasture, remembered something, and turned back to the farm. Not that it mattered.

That was a hollow walk; along the road by Bosky Wood; down the lane to the farm. Hollow. That's how I felt. Hollow, because no solution existed to Eric's disappearance. No matter where my feet took me, I would find nothing that could help. No matter what I thought; no matter what I said, who I told; the loudness of my weeping or the depth of my mourning; no solution existed.

At the sight of Eric's Mercedes in the farmyard my tears threatened to become howls. Hammering echoed under the roof. Mr Grimshaw's head poked up among the roof's tiles. He looked down at someone beside him in the loft.

"Here they are now," he said, loud enough to be talking to Bernie. But I got the impression he wasn't talking to Bernie. He tilted his head at us, then disappeared. Bang! Bang! Bang! went the hammer.

We walked round the back of the house, waiting for whoever was expecting us. The house door was shut. Feet sounded on the stairs.

The door opened.

For the second time that morning, I fainted.

Hands joggled my head. I was on my back, in the farmyard, grit under my fingers.

I opened my eyes.

Daniel pulled me to my feet.

He said nothing, but his grin told me that I wasn't seeing things.

Behind Daniel, staring anxiously at me, was Eric Railford.

He said, "Have you two been crying?"

My mouth stretched. No wonder Daniel was grinning.

"Are you ill?" demanded Eric, glancing at where I'd been sprawled.

I flew at him. I enclosed his head in my arms and kissed him with as much force as I'd kissed Daniel in the barn; but in welcome; and in joy.

"Hold on!" he said, so I held on, until he had to push me away.

Daniel was still grinning, tears dribbling down his cheeks.

Eric gazed at us, then handed me my hat. "You left it on the sacks of cattle feed," he said.

But I ignored the hat, and went on grinning, so Eric plonked it on my head.

"Have you two gone round the bend?" he asked.

"No," whispered Daniel. "Not us. You."

I folded over.

I laughed.

I laughed until I was crying again.

And Daniel laughed.

We were still laughing when Eric shoved us into the back of the Mercedes, tooted at the house, and swung the car down the lane.

Then I felt sick. I wished we'd stopped to accept Mr Grimshaw's offer of tea. I sprawled free of Daniel.

"You're not ill?" said Eric over his shoulder.

"Don't you know what happened?" I gasped.

"Yes. I went into the hay loft and you two scarpered. I assumed that three had suddenly become a crowd—"

"No! Don't you know? Don't you know what happened to you?"

"Apart from hitting my shins a couple of times," murmured Eric, "nothing happened to me. I went to Grimshaw's to wait for you—"

Daniel said, "He doesn't know."

"I don't know what?"

So we told him. The car swerved, and lunged to a halt. Eric faced us, and made us tell him again.

"I hit my shins," he said in his faraway voice. "I went up the ladder and instead of stepping onto the loft I struck the edge of the loft floor."

"What happened immediately before that?" I asked.

"Before? Oh, yes. The light changed. I remember hesitating halfway up the ladder. Did I say your name, Stella? The sunlight seemed to jump, and everything was darker; just a shade. Then after I glanced around the loft, I came down again, but you two had gone. Your hat, Stella, was on the sacks. I looked about outside, then headed back towards the farm. The sunlight was different—"

"But the barn was the same?" asked Daniel.

"Yes…"

"And the bridge?"

"Oh, yes. Everything was the same. Though the last step on the ladder broke under my weight and turned to dust. Woodworm, I suppose. I walked over the mound. I thought I'd stepped into a rabbit hole, because suddenly I went down, like going down an unexpected step on a staircase, and hit my shins on a stone. That's right, then the sun was bright again. I hopped over the iron gate—"

"We were behind you," I said. "Then you turned up the lane to the farm."

"I'd only got upstairs to ask Grimshaw if you were there, when you appeared. No wonder you fainted, Stella. I feel a bit shocked myself." Eric kinked a smile at us from the front seat of the car. "I've been in The Place Between."

Eric turned from us, and drove slowly. He said nothing.

I guessed he was picturing The Place Between, trying to remember if it was different from here.

"It's about thirty centimetres higher than this world," said Eric. "Around the barn, anyway. Which is why I bumped my shins going up into the loft. Then at the mound, I stumbled down, back into the lower level of this world."

I nodded at his back. He'd been thinking the same thoughts as me.

Then he said, "Bernie Kemp's man must have disappeared and reappeared – just like I did – when they were felling the trees on the mound."

Daniel asked Eric to explain, because we hadn't heard about the trees being cut down, but Eric said he would show us Mrs Grimshaw's letter when we got home.

We dodged the town and parked in the hospital car park. We headed for the loos.

After a wash, I felt fit to meet Mrs Grimshaw.

She was a white heap in the bed, with a pink-balloon face and sizzled hair. Her hands lay on the covers, like thick red animals; but she smiled when she saw Eric and Daniel. She hadn't met me other than in our shop. She smiled when Daniel introduced me. "Stella," she said, and the animals floated off the bed and enclosed my hand. "I can't thank you enough. You've grown into a beautiful young woman. How's that husband of mine? How is he taking this? And the house. How's my house? Not too bad, is it?"

"You'd be amazed," smiled Eric, "how he's getting on with the repairs. And Bernie's helping like one of the family."

"I've got a bit of burning." Mrs Grimshaw nodded towards her legs. "It's not bad. There's a cage over them to keep the blankets off."

I glanced at Eric, but he was listening to Mrs Grimshaw. My face warmed. I'd thought the cage was part of her bulk.

"...tell you about the fire? I wrote to the Queen," Mrs Grimshaw told Daniel and me, "and she passed it to Mr Railford here. Wasn't that kind? Have you met her personally?"

Eric shook his head.

"Never mind. I expect you will. I expect your mum's met the Queen," Mrs Grimshaw told me, "with that lovely car of hers. But you don't want to listen to my chatter. You want to know about them twigs in the tube."

"Yes," said Eric. "And about the fire."

"Same thing, my dear. Though the twigs have been around since Able's grandfather chopped down part of Bosky Wood."

I remembered that Able was Mr Grimshaw.

"Determined old man 'e was. Ninety years of age, and made up 'is mind to build a garage – set up a new business. Farming wasn't his only interest, you see. 'e loved building things. Not that 'e was much good at it, I'm sorry to say. But 'e had a love of wood and metal. With proper training, 'e might have done all right. But 'e wanted to build a garage – from scratch, as you might say. Timber from 'is own land, seasoned and cut by him and the family, the garage erected where the present garage is so's 'e could look out at it from the back sitting-room. I don't suppose 'e'd ever have mended a car. At ninety, what can a body do? But determined 'e was.

"So 'e got the men – Able and Bernie and a few others. They attacked the backside of Bosky with chain saws. I warned Able. 'Don't do it,' I said. 'Them trees be wicked,' I told 'im, 'and wickedness walks in Bosky.' But Able said it was all a waste of time, 'a man of Grandfather's age wanting a darn great garage.'

"He was right, of course. Darn great garage. Darn great heap o' timber set up alongside the field. Where the new barn is now. Used

Grandfather's timber for the barn eventually. You know where I mean?

"Sure you do. Bernie told you 'is story? Yes, I suppose 'e would. But 'e couldn't tell you mine, because 'e doesn't know it. And Able doesn't know it, because I never told 'im. 'e believes in nothing, my Able. More's the pity. Maybe we could've done something sooner. Fetched you in, I mean, Mr Railford, if Able had backed me."

Eric smiled.

"Grandfather said 'e wasn't scared of Bosky Wood, and could tell stories that'd make your hair stand on end. But 'e wasn't scared. Bought 'imself a saw for cutting away the undergrowth, with a blade the size of a dinner plate, and a long handle. All 'e had to do was switch it on; 'im being so old, you understand, we didn't want 'im straining himself with anything other than an electric saw. Fed it off a car battery, 'e did.

"'e took a lad with 'im, so's to make a start – and carry the battery.

"Grandfather buzzed through the briar and hazel and who-knows-what, while the lad raked it away for burning.

"The sky was heavy, and the trees rustled overhead. The lad was none too happy, being superstitious about the wood, but Grandfather was fair enjoying 'imself, even though Bosky grew darker as the day wore on, and the rushing of branches were as loud as angry voices.

"The idea, you see, was to clear around the foot of the trees that grew at the edge of the wood; but Grandfather never stuck to plain common sense, so 'e just followed the saw, telling the lad to stop complaining; slicing deeper into Bosky.

"'e stopped for a rest. The lad had raked away the cut undergrowth. 'e stuffed it into a sack, there being no way in for a trailer, what with roots and stones; and 'e took the sack out of the wood, leaving Grandfather alone.

"Now here's the strange thing. Grandfather says the lad never came back. The lad says Grandfather went off without him.

"Grandfather sat on a stone until the cold seeped into 'im, then went on sawing; but clearing the debris was too much for 'im, so 'e stopped work – cursing the good-for-nothing help these days.

"The good-for-nothing help was at the farm asking if Grandfather hadn't returned. And give the lad 'is due, 'e was worried. Then Grandfather appeared, cursing and raging, and the lad protested that 'e'd gone straight to where they was working after emptying the sack; but Grandfather had gone, the saw and battery along with 'im. The row was awful, for the lad wouldn't back down, and anybody could see 'e was telling the truth. But he got 'is books, 'cos Grandfather couldn't stand the sight of 'im after that. Which was a shame.

"But I'm getting ahead of myself. Grandfather was for going straight to work again with a different man to help 'im, but I remember forcing 'im to sit down to proper food and a drop of Scotch. Then 'e went back – by 'imself, because the men were busy, though one of them would follow when 'e could.

"So Grandfather was sawing in Bosky. You can imagine the gloom late in the day, when the saw stopped – and the whole roof of Bosky was heaving with voices.

"That's what it sounded like to Grandfather. But 'e wasn't scared of a noise, though 'e admitted to me that 'e'd looked around a few times, feeling that 'e was being watched.

"Then 'e saw someone.

"He assumed it was the man coming to help. He glimpsed him through the trees, approaching along the cleared path.

Now Grandfather's eyes weren't bad, but neither were they a hundred per cent; and he could only see the fellow's top half, with plenty of branches hindering his view; but Grandfather swore he was in fancy dress – like he was got up for an Elizabethan play.

"So 'e shouts, 'What are ye dressed up for? This way, man. I hope ye brought a sack!' Or words to that effect. Then Grandfather was startled, for it seemed as if the spirits of the trees had arrived at 'is call, tall and spindly, filling the cleared path, trapping 'im in Bosky Wood, and whispering. But – as I say – 'e was a determined old man. So 'e switched on the saw and buzzed at those twig-like things, ripping through them so they collapsed.

"Grandfather admitted to me that 'e was real shaken, but determined not to show it, for 'e thought his man was nearby.

"But the man wasn't nearby. Grandfather – still swinging the saw – took a step towards where the man was approaching, but found 'e was cutting empty air, and the man was nowhere among the trees.

"Well. Two men disappearing was enough even for Grandfather. 'e came back to the farmhouse. 'e said nothing then, except to ask which man had come to help 'im, and only grunted when 'e heard that no one had come. Later, 'e gave me the wooden tube 'e'd made as a boy, and told me to keep safe the twigs inside, because they were the things 'e'd cut with the saw – the things that haunted Bosky Wood. After that, he attacked the trees as if 'e hated them. 'e died before the timber was seasoned enough to build 'is garage, and now it's made into the new barn. Oh, isn't that kind! Here's the nurse with a cup of tea."

We drank the tea.

* * *

"Tell us about the fire," said Eric.

"My poor house," sighed Mrs Grimshaw. "Is Able really making a job of it?"

I said, "He's working very hard." I felt the need to say something cheering to Mrs Grimshaw, to make up for not thinking about her after the fire. Daniel's right in his attitude about caring for people. He thinks there's nothing more important. But I find even remembering to be kind so difficult.

"…house is Georgian," Mrs Grimshaw was saying, "and sometimes I walk around with just a candle, trying to imagine what it was like all them years ago.

"The night before the fire, I'd been doing just that – looking around by candlelight. Able thinks I'm touched. But 'e's got no sense of the past. When I was done wandering, I put the candlestick on the mantelpiece – in the sitting-room, where the fire started – next door to the room you found me in, Daniel. Oh, dear. Some of my best furniture was in there…!

"I'm sorry for sniffling! Is it all burned? I'm sorry. There. Don't fuss, my dears. At my age I shouldn't be so taken up with silly things like furniture.

"I'm all right now, thank you.

"I was saying… Yes. I put the candlestick on the mantelpiece and I was reading by candle-light – just for the romance of it, but eventually I snuffed the candle and went to bed.

"Late next morning, I carried a pot of tea upstairs to that room. And wasn't the country-side lovely in the sunshine! Every stalk of corn ripening beautifully! I got to thinking about the strange things that had happened – things I wrote about in my letter to the Queen – and I took the wooden tube from its drawer in the davenport. I've compared the twigs to every tree and bush in these parts but there's nothing quite like them. I don't want to touch them, mind you, because I find them unpleasant – but I have to look, my dears. I've stared hard enough over the years to wear the blessed things away.

"However, I was about to unscrew the tube when a chill blew across my neck.

"You know, I couldn't think! Even if someone'd opened the door, there was no cold air on such a hot morning; and when I looked, the door was shut – but I shivered.

"You read about rooms turning cold when ghosts are about – and as I say, queer things had happened recently, so I was prepared in my mind, and ready not to be scared.

"The candle was on the mantelpiece where I'd left it the night before. Sunlight streamed onto the mantelpiece so that I could see the candle – plain as plain – with the wick, bent and black. Then I stared, for it seemed that a spot of fiery colour glowed on the tip of the wick. I was certain it wasn't a trick of the sunlight.

"I crossed to the mantelpiece.

"Because of the sunlight, I hadn't seen what was really happening: a flame was burning on the wick.

"While I had watched, someone – without showing himself – had lit the candle."

Mrs Grimshaw relaxed, closing her eyes.

"Someone?" said Eric.

"I've never heard of a ghost lighting candles." She opened her eyes.

"So," said Eric, smiling with surprise, "you thought it was a real person?"

"Don't you think so?"

"I do, as a matter of fact," murmured Eric. "I've had a lot of experience of ghosts, Mrs Grimshaw, and do you know? The more I find out, the less sure I am that real ghosts exist. Though some very strange things do exist. But we won't go into that. Tell us what happened next."

"My own silly fault," sighed Mrs Grimshaw. "I'm sorry. I'm getting tired. But don't go, Mr Railford. This will only take a minute.

"I picked up the candlestick, to make sure – I suppose – that the candle really was lit. I even passed my hand over the flame; so it certainly was burning. Then as I bent to blow it out, a man walked across the room.

"You know how – when you're startled – you think several things very fast? Well, I thought it was Able in his shirt sleeves. Then I thought,

137

he's thinner than Able. Then I thought, where did he come from? because – of course – the door was shut. Then I wondered where he was headed, for there was nothing in front of him but my display cabinet. Is he a burglar, I wondered, helping himself to my best china? All that nonsense went through my head in a moment. My final idea was that something peculiar was happening – and something peculiar did happen – he walked clean through my display cabinet and vanished into the wall.

"I said I was ready not to be scared, but I was that startled, I shrieked and jerked around to see where he'd got to, you know, not believing what I'd seen. The candle dropped off the candlestick, though I didn't notice at the time. It landed on a cushion on an armchair. I suppose I gaped for half a minute before it dawned on me that I could smell burning. The cushion was alight, and so was my lovely chair. I tried to beat the fire out, but sparks spread onto the curtains, and there was so much smoke, and it was all too much! I ran into the next room and shut the door. There's a phone there, but the smoke was in my lungs, and I didn't reach it…! Mr Railford…!"

"Take it easy, Mrs Grimshaw," murmured Eric. "Everything's fine. You rest now. And thanks for telling us about the fire. I'll ask the nurse to look in on you. Shut your eyes. That's

138

right. We'll see you later, and I promise to do my best to clear up this mystery of Bosky Wood. OK? We'll maybe see you tomorrow."

Eric beckoned us with his eyebrows, and we whispered our goodbyes, then escaped from the hospital.

CHAPTER ELEVEN

Eric surprised us by bombing the Mercedes into the Mitre car park, and inviting us to lunch (on him).

He led us briskly through the Mitre, into the lounge, and strode towards a table with a RESERVED sign.

He looked at his watch and told the waitress we would order shortly. He said to us, "I told your mother I'd ask you along for a bite of food."

So we chatted, and the minutes drove on. Eric looked at his watch several times. He said, "She's not usually late, is she?"

"Not unless she's got a customer. What time did she say she'd come?"

"Half past one." Eric drummed his fingers.

We waited, enjoying the comfort of the Mitre lounge.

"The Place Between," murmured Eric.

"What?" I said.

"I said, 'The Place Between'. The name's appropriate, I suppose, for your friend, Susie – seeing that it came between her and this world – but not otherwise."

He sat, his charcoal hair ruffled, his face relaxed. I could almost hear his brain clicking.

"Another way of looking at it," he said suddenly, "is that it's another dimension, and not another world."

"What's the difference?" asked Daniel.

"I suppose another word for 'dimension' is 'measurement'," said Eric. "A rectangle has two measurements – length and breadth, and a box has three – length, breadth and depth."

"It's three-dimensional," I said brilliantly.

"Mm," agreed Eric. "But it has a fourth dimension, and that is time."

"Time?" said Daniel.

"Yes. Say you made a box on January the first—"

"Uh."

"It will still exist on January the second. Then it will go on existing into February. Then into the following year, and so on. In other words, it exists through time."

"Ye-es," I said, though it seemed too obvious to be worth calling a dimension.

"We can measure how long it lasts – a measurement – or dimension – of time," said Eric.

"You mean its age," I said.

Daniel said, "So everything has four dimensions?"

"Yes." Eric sounded doubtful.

Then he said, "Or possibly five."

"Five!" Daniel smiled. "I've never seen a five-dimensional box."

"That may be because we don't have the right equipment to see it with. We can understand the box's four dimensions, because we have eyes and fingers and memory – memory lets us know that the box existed yesterday," he explained, noticing my dazed look, "but we don't have the faculty to perceive the fifth dimension – but that doesn't mean it isn't there. In fact, the more I learn about The Place Between, the more I think that it may *be* the fifth dimension."

"Why?" asked Daniel.

"Because Grimshaw's new barn is in The Place Between, as well as in this world. Ebenezer's sow – four hundred years ago – seemed to find its own sty in The Place Between, while its real sty was still here. So it may be that every object in our world extends into The Place Between…"

"Oh, sh-orts!" I said. "You're not serious! Does that mean there's another Stella wandering around – ?"

Eric laughed. "I doubt it. Higher life forms don't replicate, Stella, because life is exclusive to each creature."

I wasn't sure I understood, but I was glad that replica Stellas and Daniels didn't exist.

"The only life in The Place Between," said Eric, "as far as Ebenezer Bagge could tell – and as far as I know from my investigations – is the twigs."

I looked at Daniel. I hated to think of another Stella having exactly my feelings.

Eric was fingering his watch.

"What if I bake a cake?" I demanded. Eric looked at me. "Does it pop into existence in this other dimension – "

Eric began to nod.

" – then disappear bite by bite as we eat it?"

He shook his head, laughing. "I don't know, Stella. Though it's a good question. If it doesn't disappear then the parallel world must be knee-deep in cakes."

Silence.

"Though with time being different… "

"What?"

"The sow gave us a clue to that, Stella. Pigs don't usually live for four hundred years, so if the sow is still snuffling around Upper Saxtead today, that means that only a few years – or months – have passed since Ebenezer sent it into The Place Between."

"Or minutes," suggested Daniel.

"Mm."

Eric sighed. He looked towards the door. "Then there's the artist," he said.

"Artist?" said Daniel.

"Last year. He painted Bosky Wood. I brought his easel and paintings home for you."

"What's he got to do with it?" I asked. "Mr Grimshaw said he went off in a huff because Mrs Grimshaw wouldn't buy his pictures."

"He went off, all right," agreed Eric. "Mrs Grimshaw told me about her encounter with him, when I saw her the first day I got here. Yesterday? Goodness gracious. Just yesterday.

"John Gunner was his name. He lived alone in Hammersmith."

Daniel frowned. "Did Mrs Grimshaw know all this?"

"As I told you, Daniel, the police keep me informed." Eric smiled, as if the police keeping him informed was an embarrassment. "However," he continued, "John Gunner wasn't particularly sociable, and nobody missed him for weeks. Apparently, he was in the habit of travelling about the country, painting. He never told anybody where he was going because he had no special friends, and besides, he never knew, himself, where he might end up.

"The police did look for him after he disappeared, but – as I say – he might have been anywhere. So there was no investigation around here. Mrs Grimshaw – naturally – didn't report him missing because – as you say, Stella – she thought he'd gone off in a huff.

"And he's still missing. The last person who

definitely saw him was Mrs Grimshaw. And the last place she saw him was in the pasture beside Bosky Wood. Now. Where do you think he might be? Stella?"

Dim-witted pause at our table. Then –

"I know!" I yelped. "He's in The Place Between! He could have walked into it, just as you did in the new barn! Only *he* didn't walk out again!"

Eric was looking at his watch. "Twenty minutes," he muttered uneasily. "Yes, Stella, that is a possibility."

"But you said yourself," Daniel pointed out, "he could be anywhere."

"John Gunner was dedicated to his painting, Daniel. Despite Mrs Grimshaw's disparagement of his work, the man could paint well. He wouldn't have left his equipment. I've instigated a nationwide search, anyway, just to be sure; though I'm pretty certain that he was spotted as recently as this morning, in this area." He stared straight at me.

"What!" I sat up.

"I think," said Eric, tapping nervously on his watch, "that the man we searched for in Grimshaw's barn this morning was John Gunner. I think that he walked into this world – giving you two a glimpse of him – then, not noticing us, wandered into the barn, and at some point stepped back into The Place Between."

"The man in shirt sleeves!" I yelled. Several customers raised their faces, and I whispered, "The man in shirt sleeves?"

"He lit Mrs Grimshaw's candle," said Eric, looking past me to the door, "possibly to catch her attention. And – " as I opened my mouth " – he is five feet six inches tall with blue eyes."

"The spook in my bedroom?" I squeaked.

"And the man in the square," said Eric.

"The—?"

"You saw him yesterday, Stella, in the square, then later you saw him – or his eye – in your bedroom. It looks as if he followed you, doesn't it?"

"Followed me!"

"Trying to make contact, I expect."

"But how *could* I see him," I cried, "if he was trapped in The Place Between?"

"Susie Kelso saw into The Place Between at Cromer. Mrs Grimshaw saw in when she watched John Gunner crossing her sitting-room. Perhaps Daniel saw in when the twigs followed him to your door – unless the twigs had ventured into this world, of course, which they did in Ebenezer's time. Hundreds of people have seen into The Place Between over the centuries. In fact – if my theories are correct – just about anyone who has seen a ghost was looking into The Place Between. Though there may be other explanations for ghosts too... So it seems obvious," said Eric,

146

"that the edges of The Place Between some-times fade into our world, not only letting us see in, but letting anyone there see us.

"And also: remember that The Place Between is virtually identical to this world. I doubt if John Gunner knows that he is not in dear old England at all – he's simply wondering where everybody has got to. And if – " Eric stared at a waitress gazing around the room. " – if we are right in saying that time is different… Though I didn't notice it in my short journey from the new barn to the mound…"

"Changes in time!" breathed Daniel.

"…then it's possible that John Gunner doesn't know he's been missing for a year…" He watched the waitress approach our table. "Which would account, also, for his strange behaviour in the square. Einstein's theory of relativity says that two people living at different speeds will see each other as moving very fast. Gunner probably saw you, Stella, the way you saw him…"

He stared up at the waitress.

She said, "Miss Stella Lane?"

"Yes?" I said, wondering what was coming.

"Phone call, dear. At reception. Sounds a bit urgent."

Eric stood up. I pulled my fingers from Daniel's grasp, and hurried to reception. I snatched up the phone. A clock on the wall showed three minutes to two.

"Hello?"

"Stella? Thank goodness you're there. Your mother said you might be. It's Mr Hilary, here. You'd better get home quick. Something's happened—"

"Is it Mum?" I gasped.

" – and bring that Mr Railford if he's with you! He's the only one who seems to know what's going on in this town!"

"Mr Hilary—"

"Hurry, Stella!" gasped the grocer. "I don't like being in your shop alone!" He hung up.

What did he mean, I wondered, being in our shop alone? Mum should be there. Or on her way to the Mitre to meet Eric.

I turned from the phone and found my face at Eric's chest.

"What's wrong, Stella?"

"It was Mr Hilary. He sounded in a panic. We've got to get home!"

"But what did he say?" demanded Eric. Daniel appeared and we hurried towards the car park.

"He said he didn't like being alone in our shop."

"Alone? I don't like the sound of this! I've had a bad feeling for the last half hour. Get in, kids. Seat belts on."

Eric drove like a stunt man. In no time, we skidded against the kerb in front of our shop.

Mr Hilary was waiting outside the shop

door. He led us inside, saying, "I didn't know what to do!"

"Tell us what's wrong," said Eric.

"It's Elaine!" Mr Hilary's hands waved – as if causing a draught helped make things clearer. "I just don't know!"

"Mr Hilary – what happened?" Eric sounded calm, but his face was white.

I wanted to scream at the grocer to hurry him, for his mouth opened and shut, but only his breath came out.

Then: "She was here – by that desk. And laughing over the knobkerrie. Y'know how heavy it is, and her swinging it around like a stick of rhubarb. She'd brought it from the kitchen and was going to put it back in its place on the mantelpiece. Oh! I'll need to sit down. Oh, my! Oh, my goodness! Oh, great God in Heaven! Stella, Stella, something stepped out of the wall and swept her away!"

CHAPTER TWELVE

Tears blotted my view of Mr Hilary's frightened face.

Eric ran towards the fireplace. I knew what he was trying to do, and I ran at his back. But The Place Between didn't swallow us up. We stopped against the mantelpiece.

"She's got the knobkerrie!" I whispered desperately.

"D'you know what's happening?" gasped Mr Hilary.

"Take it easy, Mr Hilary," said Daniel. He looked at Eric.

"What can we do?" I screamed.

"Be quiet, Stella. Mr Hilary. You said something swept her away. Do you mean a person? An animal?"

The grocer gaped, panting. "I can't think! I don't know what I saw! I don't know if I saw

anything! But something must have... Elaine...
She seemed to be pulled into nowhere. I can't
think!"

"What pulled her?!" I yelled. "Mr Hilary—!"

"I'm trying! Wait. She turned away from me,
the knobkerrie in both hands. She got to there,
beside that desk. Wait, now. She seemed to fall.
That's what happened. She seemed to stumble.
She said, 'Oh!' and she clutched the knobkerrie
to her chest; she put up her right hand to save
herself. Her arm disappeared. Her knees bent,
and she fell, she fell into nothingness. I don't
understand."

Mr Hilary's face quivered. "It was as if something had pulled her into the wall. Perhaps there
was nothing. I can't think. I can't think."

"You've done well, Mr Hilary," said Eric
grimly. He slid a phone from his pocket, and
dabbed a number.

"This is Brigadier Railford speaking. You
know who I am? Put me through to Inspector
Brand. Quick as you can, please... Hello,
Brand? Mrs Lane has disappeared. That's right.
As far as I know the activity is restricted to this
county... Let's say I have no reason to believe
she could reappear very far away, but if she
doesn't turn up... We'll give her an hour...
You've got her description. Good man." He
pocketed the phone.

"What happens in an hour?" I asked.

"We widen the search. But we'll find her close

by. You realize what's happened?"

I opened my mouth, but he rattled on anyway, I think partly to clear his own mind, as well as to be certain that we knew.

"The Place Between is sometimes on a different level from here – as I found at the new barn. Your mother fell down into it. Probably just a step down. I doubt if anything pulled her. As I've said, as far as we know, nothing lives in The Place Between other than our twiggy friends – and, of course, whoever slips into it out of this world. Sorry, Mr Hilary, but I think you were rationalizing something you couldn't understand when you said that something pulled her.

"Stella, your mum should reappear between here and Bosky Wood. Chances are we won't need to widen the search. Right now Daniel and I are going to look for her. Watch out if you stumble, Daniel. I don't want you falling in—"

"If we don't go in," said Daniel with a dangerous glitter, "how do we get Mrs Lane out?"

Eric stared at Daniel. But his eyes were focussed on his own fears. He took the phone again from his pocket, and touched numbers.

"Colonel McDairmid, please. Colonel, this is Brigadier Railford. Set up Phase One, will you? Yes, I'm afraid so. I'll meet you at Bosky Wood in fifteen minutes." He looked at me as he put the phone away. "Stella, I want you to stay here. In the shop. Keep your eyes peeled. There may be no change that you can see, but possibly the light will be different, or—"

"But what do I *do*?" I wailed.

"If The Place Between appears, reach into it with something. A window pole. Anything. I know it isn't very scientific but it's our only hope. Maybe your mother will be nearby and see it and find her way out. The number of this phone – " he patted his pocket " – is on the note pad in your mother's kitchen. Whatever you do – " and his look said that he couldn't bear to lose me as well " – *don't go into The Place Between*. Mr Hilary?" The grocer was less panic-stricken now that Eric was giving orders. "Would you help Daniel search for Elaine between here and Bosky Wood?"

"Of course. But she disappeared here—"

"There's no time to explain—"

Daniel interrupted quietly with, "What's Phase One?" And for dragging seconds Eric stood silent.

He gazed at me.

He said, "It's the first step in closing the door to the other universe." He added gently, "I know what I'm doing."

Then he was gone.

The Mercedes roared while the shop bell still jangled.

Then Daniel squeezed my hand, and took

Mr Hilary away to begin the search, and I stood alone, with the sun blistering in through the windows, creating a haze for the furniture to lurk behind, like angular beasts waiting for me to turn my back.

I said, "Mum," quietly.

My head felt as if steam were building up inside my skull. I knew the only thing that would release the steam would be finding my mother – and finding her while the door to The Place Between remained open.

Eric had left before I could think; roaring in his Mercedes towards Bosky Wood – before I could demand to know why he was closing the door, when my mother was still on the wrong side! and why he had sent Daniel away from me. Mr Hilary was looking for Mum outside, and so were the police. Couldn't Daniel have stayed? Then I realized that only one person was needed to watch the small area of the shop, and the more people searching outside the better the chance of finding my mother.

But here I was, by myself, with all this ancient furniture and only the smell of polish and the tick of the longcase clock for company.

A woman walked past outside, and loneliness submerged me; as if I was already in a place between, where no one could understand how I felt, and no one could reach me.

Eric had said to keep alert. For a change in the light? Or— ? He had been going to say something else, but I had interrupted him. I made up my mind to watch and listen for the slightest thing that might be strange.

I stared at the fireplace where my mother had vanished. I shut my eyes, and stood tall, refusing to cry.

Then I wandered, keeping close to the shop windows.

The light didn't change.

It was creepy to think of another universe echoing this one.

"Oh, Mum! Where are you!"

I wandered through the shop, looking for any tiny change which would tell me that The Place Between was open to me. I knew that Eric had said not to go in, but I wasn't standing around here fishing with a window pole while my mother was being shut out of existence!

"Mum!" I screamed.

But my voice fell muffled amid the furniture; not that she could have heard.

I went and sat in the kitchen.

I clung to the edge of the table because I was shaking.

Then I heard the longcase clock chiming. I guessed it was striking quarter past two. Only a little more than a quarter of an hour had passed since we'd fled from the Mitre.

The longcase clock has a pretty chime. It strikes twice for the quarters; and as I sat waiting for the second stroke, I realized that it wasn't coming.

The first stroke had sounded normal, then it seemed to cut off into silence.

I sat for three seconds waiting for that next stroke. Three seconds which could mean all eternity for my mother.

During these three seconds it dawned on me that this was the odd thing I'd been waiting for – and that The Place Between had appeared!

Then I moved! Oh, how I moved! I forgot my shaking body. My hands thrust against the kitchen table. I leapt towards the door. I hauled it open and hurtled into the shop. I flung myself, yelling, at the clock.

My hands clasped its towering sides. *Ding!* tinkled from within its case.

The second part of the chime!

"Mum!" I turned.

What a silence lay in the shop.

Sunlight trickled dimly over the furniture – so unlike the healthy light of a moment before.

The longcase clock ticked slowly, emphasizing the quietness.

"Mother!"

This was The Place Between.

The delay between the chimes was caused – I guessed – by The Place Between appearing immediately after the first chime.

Was my mother here, somewhere? wondering why she was so alone? Not realizing

156

she had stepped out of her own world?

"MUM!" I screamed.

I hadn't dared move. If I stepped away from the clock I might find myself back in reality.

But standing still wasn't going to help Mum.

"Get going, Stella!" I snarled, and I ran through the shop. I didn't run back into reality.

"Mum! Are you here?"

I noticed that the spotlights in the windows were out.

The same furniture that waited to be sold in our real shop lounged in the shadows.

A Victorian gong was a dull sun gleaming in a smear of daylight. Yet things weren't quite the same as at home.

Some items were missing. I saw a pile of dust where an African shield had been propped against a chair leg. I frowned. A lacquered tea caddy had disintegrated, leaving just its zinc interior. I wondered if everything was crumbling in this strange world.

I reached for a sewing table, and lifted its lid. Inside were bobbins of last century's thread and a pair of rusting scissors; I dropped the lid over them, wanting to hear the reassuring slap of wood on wood. But the lid struck with a dull *whup!* and burst into dust. The table tilted as the legs collapsed, then the table hit the floor, clouding more dust around me. I gaped at the heap of powder and crumbling wood which was all that was left. Even the carpet under the table had disintegrated, exposing floorboards.

I wondered, but I didn't understand.

And I didn't care.

I had to find my mother.

I had to find her quickly, and explain where we were – if she didn't already know – then find a way out of The Place Between. Phase One – after all – would be starting soon; that is, if Eric got to Bosky Wood and met his colonel within fifteen minutes of leaving me, as he had arranged on the phone.

I supposed there was a Phase Two. I think Eric had said that Phase One was the first step. For all I knew there could be a Phase Three and Four, but again, Phase Two might shut the door; might shut us in this crumbling universe for the rest of our lives.

I hurried back to the shop kitchen.

"Mum!"

I ran upstairs and darted into the sitting-room. The furniture slept. No sound came from the street. I lifted a decanter and poured a little whisky; not that I wanted it; I just wanted to taste it; but it had no taste. A flake of glass dropped off the bottom of the decanter when I replaced it on its tray.

I went into Mum's bedroom.

I went further upstairs, to the flat Eric was renting. Silence met me, and I ran down, calling, all through the house. Then I went to

158

the back door, which is really the back door of the shop. It leads into the garage where the Rolls Royce is kept. The garage was extended years ago, to accommodate pieces of furniture requiring polishing or renovation.

I rushed into this extended place with its smells of wood and wax.

My hair tried to stand on end.

Bending over an Art Deco dining table, absorbed in conversation, were a man and a woman.

"Woodworm?" said the man in shirt sleeves.

"I don't think so," said my mum, popping into full view from behind the man. "Hello, Stella. Was that you calling? This is Mr Gunner. He's an artist. There's something odd about this table. Take a look, darling, and tell us what you think."

John Gunner was staring at me as if he'd seen a ghost.

I was staring at him.

He was definitely the man who'd followed me in the square. And his eye was absolutely the blue eye that had scared me witless in my bedroom. Eric had been spot on about that!

"I found Mr Gunner," said my mother, seeing my mouth open, "trying to get the kettle to work in the shop kitchen."

The artist pulled his gaze from me.

He muttered, "Come off it, Mrs Lane, I said

159

I was sorry – but your girl gave me a right old turn, moving so fast across the square – and the kettle was force of habit – I wasn't thirsty. And what with yesterday – "

Yesterday? I couldn't help wondering what had happened to the artist yesterday. He took my glance as encouragement.

"Somebody," he exclaimed, "lifted me painting gear from under me nose! In the middle of a field, I ask you! I stepped forward for a closer look at them trees—"

"Mother!" I said urgently. I really didn't want to hear this!

I groaned as the artist rattled on.

"I wanted to call the police, didn't I? So I headed for that Grimshaw woman's farm'ouse – but nobody was around. Though the door was open. I took a liberty and popped in, but the bloomin' phone was dead. An' the 'ouse was so quiet it gave me the shivers, I can tell you. Then the air got cold, like winter had come, and dark. Listen, girl. Just listen.

"I found a candle and lit it, but … it was like a candle in a bloomin' dream. The flame went out, and blow me if the candle didn't fade away – if there was a candle. I'm not sure. I'm not sure if I didn't doze off; then I walked into town. Not that I'm fond of company, but I thought the end of the world had come! There's roofs fallen in everyplace, and not a soul, and everything so dusty. Then I saw you … Stella? How you moved so quick across that square – I dunno. I couldn't keep up. But I got into this street – " He nodded towards the front of the shop. " – in time to see you coming in 'ere, so I followed, hoping to find you, but you'd gone.

"I shouted all inside the shop. I was pretty scared. You were the only human being I'd seen since yesterday." Mr Gunner shrugged. "So I searched the 'ouse. Sat on a bed for a rest, then saw you again in the bedroom. I tell you, young lady, I 'id behind a cupboard – because you were as thin as a ghost... I couldn't make head nor tail of it. Then you faded away."

"The Place Between faded away," I breathed, but Mr Gunner was too wrapped up in his story to listen.

"Then," he said, "I scrammed; found a bike and went back to the farm'ouse for another look for me easel. I even searched the barn.

"Then I thought I'd come back here, 'cos a spooky girl's better than nobody. Blooming bike collapsed under me, so I only got 'ere arf-an-hour ago. But there wasn't a soul. Then I thought I'd make meself a cuppa. But the kettle wouldn't work. Then your mum came in and nearly murdered me with that knobkerrie... Pardon me, I'm sure, but it wasn't funny—"

"I'm sorry," I gasped. "I'm not really laughing. It's nerves. I'll explain later."

This wasn't the moment to tell John Gunner that it was a year since Mrs Grimshaw had removed his equipment when he vanished from the pasture at Bosky Wood; or that it was yesterday evening he had followed me from the square and ended up in my bedroom – not this morning. Though Daniel and I *had* seen Mr Gunner walking into Grimshaw's barn this morning, but early – not late in the morning as Mr Gunner thought. Oh!

I groaned, "Let's get out of here!"

I felt the blood flowing away from my face as I recalled how little time was left. Eric *must* have begun Phase One by now!

"Stella!"

"I'm all right. But we've got to *move!* Mum," I said, quietly but urgently, "we're in The Place Between."

I knew as I spoke that it sounded crazy.

My mother looked at me, waiting to hear more.

I had to convince her quickly.

I said, "What happened to Mr Hilary?"

"He … he dashed away." Mum looked confused. "We were laughing about something – what? twenty-five minutes ago?" She turned suddenly on Mr Gunner. "I'm sorry, but I don't understand how you got into the shop without my seeing you! Into the kitchen…?"

Mr Gunner shrugged, obviously as bewildered as Mum. I said, "Mum, Mr Gunner didn't come into *our* shop at any time – "

"'Ere!" from Mr Gunner.

" – he came into *this* shop – in The Place Between! While we were still in our real shop! Now," my voice soared, "we're *all* in The Place Between!"

Mum stared at me.

Then she continued quietly. "As I was saying – Mr Hilary and I were laughing. I turned to put the knobkerrie on the mantelpiece, and I stumbled over the kerb. When I turned round again Mr Hilary had gone. I was surprised that he hadn't stepped forward to help. I didn't even hear the bell jangle on the door as he left. Then everything was so quiet. I kicked over that African shield and it turned to dust. I wasn't happy about that! I kept hold of the knobkerrie and searched the shop—"

"Came into the kitchen like a wraith, she did!" yelped Mr Gunner. "Frightened the life out of me!"

"We realized something odd was going on – Mr Gunner and I – so I thought we'd take the car and see if we could find anybody. I put the knobkerrie on this table. Look for yourself, Stella."

I looked. A corner of the table had disintegrated where the knobkerrie had bumped down.

"We're in The Place Between," I repeated.

"Everything is like that." I lifted a mallet, and with an effort, snapped off its handle.

Mr Gunner gaped, took the mallet-head from me and crushed it in his fingers. The wood powdered and streamed to the floor.

"What's goin' on!" he whispered.

Mother – in her faintest voice – said, "How do we get back?"

"I know where I came in," I said.

We hurried, Mum hefting the knobkerrie, John Gunner catching our fear and scampering with us, though he couldn't have understood. I scarcely understood either. If The Place Between really was the fifth dimension as Eric had said, then it was a pretty unstable place with everything crumbling to dust – though it would explain my question about why it wasn't knee-deep in cakes that nobody had eaten.

I strode from beside the longcase clock. Mum and Mr Gunner followed me, but nothing changed. I wasn't sure if we were back in reality or not – though the sunlight was still dim. I picked up a Toby jug and tapped it on the wall. The jug fell to pieces, and dust drifted from the wall.

I said nothing, but led my mother and the artist to the fireplace. We gathered on the hearth, and I think all three of us felt pretty foolish; but I was frightened.

This was where Mum had entered The Place

Between. We had just walked past the desk, now we were about to walk past it again in the other direction. Two steps could take us home. Or leave us stranded in this dusty universe, where – I thought – even the kettle wouldn't boil.

I took the two steps.

"Have we done it?" asked Mum.

I saw piles of dust where small objects had stood.

"Could one of you girls explain—"

"It hasn't worked!" I groaned. "What can we do! Mum? Eric's closing the door to The Place Between! He may have started by now! If we don't find the way out…"

"Doesn't he know we're here?"

"He knows you're here. He knows Mr Gunner's here!"

"Then why—?"

"He didn't take time to explain! We have to find a way to escape. Come on!"

I opened the shop door and ran into the street. "I think we should head for Bosky Wood! That's where Eric was going! He said it was the centre of activity!"

"We'll take the Rolls!"

"No, Mum. It'll be like the kettle. It won't work. And the spotlights. Nothing electrical seems to work. Only the longcase clock – I suppose, because it's mechanical! Leave the knobkerrie. Come on!"

We walked.

I jogged. Mum trotted easily, the knobkerrie resting on her shoulder. I didn't mention the knobkerrie again.

I looked at Mr Gunner, wondering if he was fit enough to cover the six miles to Bosky at this speed. I wondered if *I* was fit enough. I saved my breath by not asking.

We passed the butcher's shop where the dog slept in the doorway so that customers have to step over him. The doorway was dogless. The shop had neither customers nor assistants. And the roof had collapsed. There was dust everywhere.

We sped on.

Mr Gunner ran well. We saw no one in town. We paced along the road with hedges closing us in, guiding us through the countryside. But there was no freshness in the air.

We ran steadily.

"D'you think we're being watched?" panted Mr Gunner.

Our feet beat up dust from the road.

He was right. I looked at Mum. She looked at me and nodded.

We were more than halfway to Bosky, when Mr Gunner demanded a rest. Desperate though I was to get on, I couldn't object. Then we ran again.

"Hurry!" I gasped, picturing Eric and his

military people setting up Phase One.

And we ran faster, though the three of us were panting as if we couldn't take another step; but none of us was sweating, I noticed, and I remembered that Mr Gunner hadn't been thirsty even after a day in The Place Between.

Once, Mr Gunner staggered to a halt, hauling in air. But I nagged at him, allowing him no rest. However, the few seconds of standing still benefited our legs and lungs, and we fairly fled along the road towards Bosky Wood.

Half a mile to go.

I could see the wooden gate that led into the pasture – the gate Daniel and Susie had climbed to escape the twigs. I had ignored the feeling that we were being watched, so desperate was I to hurry – but now the feeling strengthened.

The road ran clear to the iron gate. There was Bosky Wood curving green beyond the pasture. There was Grimshaw's farm – not blackened by fire, but as good as new. Which puzzled me, because only this morning Mr Grimshaw had been busy working on the roof – he couldn't have completed it by this afternoon.

A figure dropped off the iron gate into the road.

We staggered to a halt, peering through the dim sunlight and the dust drifting from our feet.

Fear of being too late for Phase One made me

want to run; fear of a stranger in this strange world made me stand still; though again, stopping helped us recover our wind. We were still several hundred yards from the gate.

"What's 'e wearing?" gasped Mr Gunner.

"Looks like fancy dress!" panted my mother. "Shakespeare style." Then the figure urged us forward, pointing over the iron gate into the field. I saw an old domed roof beyond the hedge.

A building in the pasture? But there *was* no building.

Then we jogged – cautiously at first.

I looked at the building – thinking.

The man must have seen us from inside its dome and come out to urge us on – for some reason. But why the fancy dress?

The dome gave me a clue.

I could see that the building was on the mound. It was the building that in our world was a scatter of stones with tree stumps sticking up among them. In this world – in The Place Between – someone had maintained that building; and there was only one man who would have reason to do such a thing, because the dome was his observatory. And he wasn't wearing fancy dress; he was in his everyday clothes.

Ebenezer Bagge.

I ran fast.

My mother sped beside me, the knobkerrie bouncing on her shoulder.

Behind us panted Mr Gunner.

Ebenezer Bagge – when he saw us rushing – climbed the gate again, into the field. Beyond him, in Bosky Wood, a movement caught my eye. Ebenezer leaned over the gate and beckoned furiously. I heard his voice, but it fell thinly through the lifeless air and I couldn't catch his words.

Then he turned and vanished behind the hedge that borders the pasture; and I saw a movement again, as if a wind had stirred Bosky Wood. The trees heaved, but I didn't feel a wind, except the breeze of my running. Then from among the leafy branches appeared branches with no leaves; thin branches, as thin as the twigs in Mrs Grimshaw's wooden tube; and they advanced, towering, into the pasture, with a horrid rustling across the grass, and a whispering among their twigs, like a thousand voices carried on a wind from a distance.

Then we heard a cry.

I was startled when Mum drew ahead of me.

She reached the iron gate and was over it before I caught up.

Then I clung to the gate, my throat raw with gasping, amazed at the sight of trees being in the pasture, amazed at my mother swiping through them with the knobkerrie, clearing a path towards Ebenezer Bagge, who was hemmed in by branches.

Then the whole whispering forest retreated towards Bosky (where – I noticed – only stumps of the boundary fence showed among the undergrowth) and it seemed to me that the trees had meant no harm (how could they? having no strength?) – but as they retreated, they took Ebenezer with them; not because they wanted him, but because he was caught up in their midst.

I hauled myself over the gate, and Mr Gunner clambered beside me.

Ebenezer – in the grasp of the trees – opened his mouth, but the dust of shattered twigs (for he was threshing around with his arms) swamped him, and no sound reached us. Then I saw his hand flapping, urging us frantically towards the building on the mound.

And I knew what we had to do.

There was no time to help Ebenezer. I grabbed Mum. She dropped the knobkerrie, and we ran towards the building.

It was a brick and timber house with the observatory one storey above us.

I pushed a door open and we bundled inside.

"It's cold!" gasped Mum. "Ooh! Bitter! How can it be cold?"

I had felt this chill before – when I saw John Gunner's eye in my bedroom; and I remembered what Eric had told me.

"Energy's being transferred!" I gasped. "Like a fridge gives off heat to make it cold inside! It means something's going to happen! What do we do? Which room? There's no time!"

Then I thought of the observatory and raced up an iron staircase. It seemed an odd site for an observatory – close to Bosky Wood, rather than on a hilltop. But the circular room at the top of the stair had no telescope; it was crowded with strange optical instruments, modern in purpose, it seemed, but Elizabethan in design, and these instruments, even now, gathered sunlight, and flashed patterns of brightness all around the room.

I looked from a window down onto the pasture. I shrieked, and Mum and Mr Gunner came beside me.

On the pasture, as faint as if on the edge of a dream, stood Daniel, Eric and a spread of soldiers. The soldiers were attending instruments. Eric's arm was raised. A laser beam appeared, unhindered by the solid walls around us.

"Phase Two!" I gasped. "There's no time left!"

Eric's arm jerked a shade higher. When his arm descended, I knew that the door to The Place Between would be shut for ever.

Fear almost dropped me to my knees. I reached for my mother, and was startled to find her gone. Mr Gunner stepped away. Things crashed to the floor behind me, though the pattern of lights didn't change. A wooden bench rushed at the window with my mum underneath it, her beautiful hands holding it high.

The bench exploded through the window. What a pity, I thought stupidly, to destroy seventeenth century glass; then my mother screamed, "Jump!"

Jump?

We were in the observatory, one storey up. It was too high to jump. She grabbed me by the scruff of my neck and the seat of my skirt, and threw me after the bench. The universe blurred. I spun head-first, cold air on my palms. I think I was silent as I fell, trying to judge where the ground was, trying to somersault to land on my feet; trying to see or hear if Mum and Mr Gunner were following; trying to see if Eric had dropped his arm in the signal that would seal The Place Between.

I landed on one foot and rolled on the grass as swiftly as a bottle down a hill. I couldn't stop myself. I heard yells. I heard Eric's voice – his blessed! beloved! voice! Then I hit something soft and all the breath went out of me, and my head floated with splashes of light. A man was talking in my ear, calm words. I think he was holding my arms to keep me from hitting him. His uniform was rough. He was the something soft I'd rolled into.

Then solid real hands lifted me to my feet, and Daniel's face arrived before me. His cheeks were thin. His hair was too long. I didn't understand. I heard Mum's voice. Daniel's anorak was zipped tight to his neck. John Gunner asked a question.

"Daniel!" I whispered.

He lunged at me and hugged me oh, so close! I could feel him weeping.

Mum's voice rang accusingly: "Why did you close the door? Eric Railford! You knew I was in there! Why didn't you wait?" And so on; but I just clung to my lovely Daniel.

Then quietness spread around us.

I eased my face from Daniel's cheek.

Mum was gaping past Eric. Eric was wrapped warmly in an army greatcoat.

John Gunner sat down on the grass, stunned, a pile of splinters beside him that had been a bench – until Mum had hurled it through the observatory window. Behind the artist, the mound was just the mound, with its stones and tree stumps – and a scatter of white rags.

I didn't understand. The grass of the pasture straggled thick and dark as winter, strewn with more white rags. And the trees of Bosky Wood held leafless limbs to the sky; and I saw that the sky was rushing with storm clouds, and I knew then, that the rags were snow.

I turned in fear, to Daniel.

He whispered, "You've been gone four months."

EPILOGUE

In April of the following year, we invited Mr Gunner to the wedding, but he excused himself, saying his ankle was still sore, but thanks for returning his easel and paintings. Madge Roper was there, appearing on the cathedral steps, almost as well-dressed as my mother. Mr Hilary and his daughter, Daisy, arrived, wearing good clothes carefully – like tailored cardboard.

Daniel's mother descended from a hired Daimler (with his dad) and couldn't have been more proud if the Queen had invited her. We were pleased that Mr and Mrs Grimshaw had come, and dear Bernie Kemp, who smiled his shy smile and searched the air with his right ear when anyone spoke.

Mum was there, of course, utterly stunning, and being photographed by everything from the local paper to the society mags. She was photographed with Eric (magnificent in his brigadier's dress uniform); she was photographed without Eric. She was photographed with me (pretty gorgeous, I admit, in a hot little number from Madge's boutique – I never did discover the price of that jacket in Jenner's). But Mother was the real centre of attention. And why not?

It was her wedding day.

I don't think anyone quite believed it. I mean, about The Place Between. I didn't, and I had been there – for four months – or an hour.

And Mum had forgiven Eric for putting Phase One in motion.

Phase One, it turned out, took a week to set up – optical instruments and lasers – the modern equivalent of the lenses and mirrors in Ebenezer's observatory. Eric would not allow Phase Two to be activated until a scrupulous search had been made for us, but there was an increased presence of The Place Between, and one or two people had disappeared. We hadn't seen them, but – as Eric said – they could have ended up anywhere – or any time.

Eventually, on the 20th of December, Eric – under pressure from his bosses in the government – reluctantly decided to activate Phase Two. He had given up hope of seeing Mum and me again.

His biggest shock – and greatest happiness –

was when we fell out of thin air just as he dropped his arm to signal the closing of the door.

John Gunner broke his ankle when he jumped with us – though nobody noticed for ten minutes, including Mr Gunner. Mum had landed without a scratch. I had bruises from shoulder to shin.

Eric could hardly believe that Ebenezer had succeeded in setting up an escape route using unreliable sunlight inside the observatory. (Rather than steady artificial light which, of course, was unavailable in The Place Between.) But Ebenezer, fortunately, *had* used sunlight because we wouldn't have got home otherwise. Eric reckoned that Ebenezer had made many attempts to escape and these were the cause of the increased phenomena in this world, with The Place Between coming and going quite out of anyone's control.

And *I* guessed that Ebenezer had seen Mum and Mr Gunner and me running along the road towards Bosky Wood just as his instruments had opened the door into the real world, so he had hurried out to beckon us on, to take us with him. He maybe even saw Eric and his soldiers setting up their instruments, and guessed that they were about to close the door. I was amazed at Ebenezer's unselfishness – he had given up everything for three people he didn't know.

And Eric isn't finished, yet, with The Place Between.

The jar of twigs that he sent for analysis contained nothing but dust when it arrived, so somebody chucked it out; but Eric intends discovering how to control the opening and closing of the door, and therefore getting a chance to study this strange twiggy life form. He also intends possibly rescuing people who have disappeared over the years – or (incredible thought!) over the centuries. So maybe we'll meet Ebenezer again one day and be able to say thank you.

But all that is a long way off.

And so is Eric – with my Mum. On their honeymoon.

A gentleman from London is looking after the shop while they're away. Eric brought him in during our four months in The Place Between to maintain Mum's business, then invited him back for the honeymoon.

(You know what I mean.)

One of my problems, now, is that I don't know how old I am. I mean, have I lost four months of my life by being in The Place Between? or have I gained four months?

Mum insists that we're both four months younger – though I don't know how she worked that out!

Anyway we did have a marvellous coming-home party at Grimshaw's farm at Christmas (celebrating a birthday that Mum missed while we were gone) and we were both absolutely laden with presents, including a rather special ring for me from Daniel. Not an engagement ring, because we're both too young – but the ring certainly has a promise in it, I think, for the future.

So I certainly don't *feel* four months too young.

SOMETHING WATCHING

Hugh Scott

Beyond the table, something reared. Two tiny dots of light stared at Alice. The thing had grown. In its blackness she saw faint patterns of paw prints on sand...

Alice first sees the leopard-skin coat when her mother is clearing out the loft, ready for the family's move to an old castle – and it makes her shudder. Attached to the coat is a label insisting that it be burned, but without explanation. It soon becomes obvious, though, that something evil has been unleashed. Something monstrous. Something that means the family harm.

"A chilling tale in true gothic style, building to a spine-chilling climax."
The Times

WHY WEEPS THE BROGAN?

Hugh Scott

WED. 4 YEARS 81 DAYS FROM HOSTILITIES...
so reads the date on the clock in central
hall.

For Saxon and Gilbert, though, it's just
another day in their ritualized indoor
existence. Saxon bakes, Gilbert brushes,
together they visit the Irradiated Food
Store, guarding against spiders. Among
the dusty display cases, however, a far
more disturbing creature moves...

But what *is* the Brogan? And why does it
weep?

"Deftly evoked, the narrative is cleverly
constructed, and there is no denying the
nightmarish power of the story. There is a
true shock ending." *The Listener*

"A very compelling and very interesting
book."
Jill Paton Walsh
The Times Educational Supplement

A Whitbread Novel Award Winner
Shortlisted for the McVitie's Prize

THE HAUNTED SAND

Hugh Scott

"Murder, Frisby! Murder on the beach!"

There's something creepy in the church-yard. There's something deathly down on the sand. Darren feels it, Frisby hears it, George thinks it's a bit of a laugh. But there's nothing funny about murder...

"Intriguing ingredients abound: a haunted church; fearful chases; ghostly weeping; skulls; bronze helmets; gems and The Black Death... Rendellesque subtleties of storyline build to an unforeseen climax."
The Times Educational Supplement

QUEST

David Skipper

"Be careful, Tom. Your power is growing. It shines like the Golden Star…"

The pocket watch is the key to it all. Tom got it from an old tinker a couple of years ago, the day before his parents were killed in a boating tragedy. Now the watch is going backwards, and Tom and his friend Douglas are in another world. Their arrival there is no accident; Tom has been called to undertake a thrilling, vital and extremely dangerous quest. A quest that will bring him into direct conflict with the evil and powerful Prince Aldred.

CALABRIAN QUEST

Geoffrey Trease

Her heart nearly stopped... The figure was human – but the head upturned to meet her incredulous stare was the head of a wolf.

A fifth-century Roman christening spoon is the catalyst for this thrilling adventure which sees Max, a young American, travel to Italy with Andy, Karen and her cousin Julie on a quest for lost treasure. It's not long, though, before they encounter some sinister happenings and find themselves in conflict with the local Mafia...

"A gripping story of archaeological adventure... The tale rattles along, demonstrating an unputdownability as durable as [Geoffrey Trease] himself."
Mary Hoffman, The Sunday Telegraph

"From storytelling such as this, readers are infected with a love of books."
Jill Paton Walsh
The Times Educational Supplement

SONG FOR A TATTERED FLAG

Geoffrey Trease

The time is December 1989.
The place, Romania.
The event, revolution!

The last leg of his school orchestra's concert tour brings eighteen-year-old Greg Byrne to Bucharest, Romania – his mother's homeland – where he hopes to make contact with a distant cousin, Nadia. But the city, as Greg quickly discovers, is a dangerous, fearful place, held in the iron grip of dictator Nicolae Ceausescu and his dreaded Securitate. What Greg cannot know, though, is that he and Nadia are about to be involved in one of the greatest events of modern history!

"Ingenious plotting... Vivid."
The Times Educational Supplement

WOLFSONG

Enid Richemont

His cheek was smooth against mine, his satin-sleek hair slicked across my skin. "C'est impossible," he whispered...

Chanteloup, "wolf song", is the name of the old mansion in Brittany where Ellie stays one summer with her mum, sister and best friend, Amy, as guests of Martine and her son Angus. Every room is filled with relics from former days – none more striking than the old photograph, above Ellie's bed, of a very handsome young man that any teenage girl might fantasize about. But for Ellie the fantasies soon become disturbingly real...

"Gripping." *The Daily Telegraph*

THE LAST CHILDREN

Gudrun Pausewang

It's the beginning of the summer holidays and the Bennewitzs are on their way to visit grandparents in the mountains. Suddenly, there's a blinding light in the sky – and the Bennewitzs are on the road to hell...

Shocking, distressing, brutally honest, this fictional account of the aftermath of a nuclear holocaust has already profoundly affected thousands of readers in Germany. Read it and it will change you too.

"This disturbing book shouldn't be limited to the teenage market but should be compulsory reading for most adults, especially those in positions of power."
Judy Allen, The Sunday Times

BACKTRACK

Peter Hunt

"*Our Correspondent in Hereford last night informed us of another shocking railway catastrophe. A train was derailed near the village of Elmcote with terrible results...*" The Times, Friday, September 3rd, 1915

When Jack and Rill meet one summer, they discover that they both had great uncles involved in an old and still unexplained railway crash. So who better to try to find out what really happened?

"A smashing mystery/thriller... If you like ideas as well as action, *Backtrack* is for you." *Weekend*

"Imaginative ... a nice astringent variant on the boy-girl motif."
The Observer

KISS THE KREMLIN GOODBYE

Alison Leonard

He didn't put his arms round her straight away, but leaned and kissed her over the space between them...

The Drama Club trip to Moscow takes a thrilling and complicated turn for Megan, when she meets the engaging Kostya, one of the stars of the Student Theatre...

Set at the time of the opening of the Berlin Wall, this is an absorbing story about young people of different cultures coming together – in friendship, fury, and understanding.

"Funny and moving ... wholly convincing."
School Librarian

THE BURNING BABY
AND OTHER GHOSTS

John Gordon

The glowing ashes turned again and then, from the centre, there arose a small entity, a little shape of fire. It had a small torso, small limbs, and a head of flame. And it walked.

A teenage girl disappears mysteriously a few days before bonfire night; two youths out skating see something grisly beneath the ice; an elderly spinster feeds her young charge to the eels... Unnatural or violent death are at the heart of these five supernatural tales, in which wronged spirits seek to exact a terrible and terrifying retribution on the living. Vivid as fire, chilling as ice, their stories will haunt you.

"All the stories include hauntingly memorable apparitions... A major collection." *Ramsey Campbell, Necrofile*

MORE WALKER PAPERBACKS

For You to Enjoy

☐ 0-7445-2308-7   *Something Watching*
by Hugh Scott   £2.99

☐ 0-7445-2040-1   *Why Weeps the Brogan?*
by Hugh Scott   £2.99

☐ 0-7445-1427-4   *The Haunted Sand*
by Hugh Scott   £2.99

☐ 0-7445-3187-X   *Quest*
by David Skipper   £3.99

☐ 0-7445-2304-4   *Calabrian Quest*
by Geoffrey Trease   £2.99

☐ 0-7445-3082-2   *Song For a Tattered Flag*
by Geoffrey Trease   £2.99

☐ 0-7445-3098-9   *Wolfsong*
by Enid Richemont   £2.99

☐ 0-7445-1750-8   *The Last Children*
by Gudrun Pausewang   £2.99

☐ 0-7445-1466-5   *Backtrack*
by Peter Hunt   £3.99

☐ 0-7445-2360-5   *Kiss the Kremlin Goodbye*
by Alison Leonard   £2.99

☐ 0-7445-3080-6   *The Burning Baby
and Other Ghosts*
by John Gordon   £2.99

**Walker Paperbacks are available from most booksellers,
or by post from B.B.C.S., P.O. Box 941, Hull, North Humberside HU1 3YQ**

24 hour telephone credit card line 01482 224626

To order, send: Title, author, ISBN number and price for each book ordered, your full
name and address, cheque or postal order payable to BBCS for the total amount and allow
the following for postage and packing: UK and BFPO: £1.00 for the first book, and 50p
for each additional book to a maximum of £3.50. Overseas and Eire: £2.00 for the first
book, £1.00 for the second and 50p for each additional book.

Prices and availability are subject to change without notice.

Name _____

Address _____

_____